MUTATION

Also by K.A. Applegate

ANIMORPHS ®

REMNANTS™

MUTATION

K.A. APPLEGATE

AN
APPLE
PAPERBACK

SCHOLASTIC INC.
New York Toronto London Auckland Sydney
Mexico City New Delhi Hong Kong Buenos Aires

ISBN 0-590-88194-9

12 11 10 9 8 7 6 5 4 3 2 1   2 3 4 5 6 7/0

Printed in the U.S.A.   40
First Scholastic printing, March 2002

For Michael and Jake

MUTATION

It didn't hurt. Not exactly.

Something was blocking the pain, but whatever anesthetic was numbing Kubrick's nerve endings, it did nothing to block the smells or sounds.

The sound of flesh being torn wetly away from his muscle in square after perfect square.

The smell of fat smoking as a laser beam burned through his skin.

The sound of his father weeping and muttering, "No, no, please, god, no."

The smell of blood.

It went on for hours. Kubrick kept his eyes closed, but he couldn't stop the images from forming in his mind. He could feel what was happening to him from a distance — the way he remembered feeling a dentist drill into one of his molars back on Earth, five hundred years ago.

He was floating in midair, suspended by some sort of invisible field, unable to move as the robotic machinery worked slowly and carefully. First the laser beam tracing the sides of a square, then a robotic arm moving in to peel back the skin.

Starting from his scalp, moving down over his face and neck, across his chest and belly, and then down his legs and feet.

He lost the hair on his head. He lost his lips, his fingers, and his toenails.

There was only one explanation. He was in hell, in purgatory, in one of Dante's circles, being punished for the wickedness of his life. Punished for stealing from his mother's purse, for hating his father.

Skinned alive.

Finally, it was done.

Several long minutes passed during which Kubrick waited, eyes squeezed shut, heart pounding. He expected somehow for it to start over again, for the robotic arm to move back to his head and begin again on his scalp. He would be like Sisyphus with his stupid rock, condemned to this one awful experience for eternity.

Instead he heard a wet sucking sound and his father's gasp. He felt a hot, dry wind on his tongue. He was lowered onto the floor. The surface pressed into his shoulder blades and butt. But, still, there was no pain.

Then — nothing. Nothing for so long, Kubrick couldn't stand the suspense any longer. Cautiously, reluctantly, stomach clenching, heaving, he opened his eyes and looked down the length of his body.

Total horror show.

His skin was completely gone. He'd known that. Yes. Felt it happening. But that wasn't the same as *seeing* it. Seeing his red muscles exposed, blue veins, startling white bones. Seeing his whole body glistening as if he'd been dipped in a clear neoprene suit.

He squeezed his eyes shut again, but it was too late to erase the image. And now his father was approaching. "Frederico, son, can you hear me?" He was weeping, doing a decent impression of someone who cared. "Are you able to get up?"

Kubrick sat up.

His father was right there, looking a bit freaky himself. Bloodshot eyes, gray complexion, pale lips. He reached out with one panicky, trembling hand and gingerly touched Kubrick on the forearm.

Kubrick jerked away. A gesture remembered from another life, but no longer necessary. He couldn't feel his father's sympathetic touch.

He couldn't feel anything.

CHAPTER ONE

"I'VE ALWAYS KNOWN THINGS."

Mo'Steel crouched, ready for action.

Things did not look good. He was trapped inside a dimly lit room with the deeply strange Billy Weir and a dead body. The body belonged to Wylson Lefkowitz-Blake. She'd been washed over the rail of the U.S.S. *Constitution* and drowned.

Dead things gave Mo'Steel the overall body shudders. At least he'd convinced Billy to stop moving Wylson like an oversized marionette. Billy could do things like that. Billy could do things that chilled Mo'Steel's soul and something told him he hadn't seen the half of it yet.

Mo'Steel's fingers itched for a weapon. He had nothing. Just the ragged clothes — now wet — he'd been wearing when Billy Weir and Wylson went overboard and he went after them.

His ears strained toward any tiny sound. A metallic grinding noise like a rusty motor came and went. Ditto an electrical snap that put Mo'Steel's nerves on edge. Water dripped from half a dozen pipes feeding into the room.

Mo'Steel could also hear something like little pops. Small sounds nearby or big sounds far away? Big sounds far away, Mo'Steel felt sure.

The sounds of battle.

Two alien species, the Blue Meanies and the Squids, fighting over a statue that looked like a primitive godhead. The humans — including his best friend and his mom — were caught in the middle.

The Blue Meanies were better fighters, more advanced. They had flying space suits, missiles, and guns that fired tiny shards of metal.

Mo'Steel knew only two things about the Squids. One: They looked like Squids, with a dozen or so arms, pink eyes, and a long bullet-shaped head. Two: They could convert matter into deadly liquid jets.

The humans were basically defenseless. Trapped on a ship they could barely control.

Mo'Steel wanted back on the ship, back in the action. He hated waiting. Waiting made every fiber of his body scream in protest. Waiting was boring and boredom was a slow death.

"Don't worry," Billy said. "Someone is coming for us."

Mo'Steel believed him. Why shouldn't Billy be able to see the future? He'd seen Billy do things that were crazy, impossible.

"When?" Mo'Steel said, easing into a sit.

"Soon."

"You think or you know?"

"I know," Billy said.

"How?" Mo'Steel had been wondering for some time how Billy did the things he did. Now seemed as good a time as any to get some answers.

"I've always known things," Billy said, troubled. He didn't seem interested in talking, but Mo'Steel felt the need to draw him out.

"What kinds of things?"

"I knew the Rock would come," Billy said.

Mo'Steel absorbed this silently. The Rock — that's what their little band of ragged survivors called the asteroid that destroyed Earth. Mo'Steel had seen it hit, seen the planet break apart like an overripe watermelon smashed by a bullet into three pieces.

The Remnants missed impact by mere hours. Just

before the asteroid hit, they'd been rushed aboard a patched-together shuttle called the *Mayflower* in a panicky attempt to save the human race.

Eighty people fled on the ancient shuttle fitted out with solar sails and hibernation berths. Many died on the journey. Mo'Steel lost his father.

Five hundred years later, the survivors, the ones who hadn't molded in their berths or gotten eaten by worms, found themselves on what first appeared to be a planet.

They now knew it was actually an immense ship. A ship run by a computer so powerful the Blue Meanies worshipped it as a god they called Mother. This computer was capable of creating environments based on data chips stored on the Remnants' shuttle.

So far, the computer had displayed malice or confusion or possibly a very twisted sense of humor. The environments it had created were creepy and often deadly.

"Something happened to me during the trip." Billy spoke without affect, and yet Mo'Steel felt a strange chill. Something happened to Billy and it had been woolly enough to leave him catatonic. He'd only recently begun to move and to talk.

"What do you mean, during the trip?" Mo'Steel

asked. "What could happen to you during five hundred years of blank nothingness, the big sleep?" For
Mo'Steel, the five-hundred-year voyage had passed
as swiftly as a night's sleep.

"I didn't sleep."

"Didn't . . ." Mo'Steel sat back and let out a low
whistle. Five centuries of insomnia. Talk about waiting. Imagine waiting five hundred years without so
much as twitching a muscle. It was the worst kind of
prison, a prison with no escape — not even offing
yourself.

"How —" Mo'Steel started to ask how Billy had
kept from losing his mind, but he let his voice trail
off. He knew the answer. Billy hadn't stayed sane.
Five hundred years of tick, tock, tick, tock without a
little action to relieve the ho-hum? Sanity wasn't an
option.

"Why were you zoned out at first?" Mo'Steel
asked.

"I think I just slowed down. Not much happening
on that long ride."

"How come you're back to normal now?"

"Don't know. Things sped up."

Mo'Steel's mind was turning. Maybe Billy could
do something, get them out of this stupid dim cell.
Get them out even though Mo'Steel couldn't see a

door. Couldn't see anything but four black metal walls, a grate floor, and dripping pipes.

"You know —" Mo'Steel hesitated, not sure of how to say this. "You know you can do stuff, right?"

"I think I can see your memories."

"Memories!" Mo'Steel laughed. What good were memories? Earth was history. And everything that had happened since they'd woken up was a nightmare. "Forget memories. You can fly! I saw you hovering over your old man."

"Did I? I wasn't sure if that was real or a dream. I'm not sure you're real, either."

"Oh, I'm real," Mo'Steel said. "And I want out of here. Got any ideas?"

"I can touch their minds," Billy said. "Touch their minds and make them come."

"Whose minds?"

Billy didn't answer.

Mo'Steel crouched down again. His ears strained. Long moments passed and then he heard them.

Voices.

Human voices.

Just outside.

CHAPTER TWO

"DETAILS AREN'T MY THING."

The battle was over. That was the good news.

The bad news was that the *Constitution* was in serious danger of swamping, capsizing, sinking.

Jobs stood unsteadily on the deck as the ship fell into the trough of a wave and rolled to starboard. Rolled and rolled and rolled . . . and rolled.

Just as Jobs was certain they were really going over, the wave started to rise under them. The ship righted itself for a few seconds. But as the wave's motion continued, they rolled just as crazily toward port.

Jobs looked up into the rigging. Sails hung in tatters. Ropes were shredded. All three masts were chewed and burned by Blue Meanie weapons. The few scraps of sails that were picking up a light wind weren't large enough to move a massive wooden warship.

The oversized statues they'd been dodging since the night before rose up here and there like bumpers on a pinball machine. Miss Blake could probably have told him the artists' names.

Jobs couldn't. He didn't know anything about art history. He did know the statues were Statue of Liberty size and constructed of solid marble. Oh, and he knew one more thing. Unless they could regain control of the helm, they were going to crash into one of them eventually.

This is my fault, Jobs told himself angrily.

He'd fallen asleep.

Fallen asleep and woken up in the pitch black to feel the ship rolling wildly, creaking eerily from the strain of simply holding together.

Weak.

He never should have given himself permission to go belowdecks after they'd escaped from the Blue Meanies. He'd found a quiet spot on one of the lower decks, laid flat on the deck so nobody would see him, and shed a few tears for Mo'Steel.

Mo'Steel had gone overboard during the battle, hours earlier. He drowned, must have drowned. Thinking there was some way he might be alive was childish, ridiculous.

Jobs had to face facts. Mo was dead. His mom

and dad were dead. Cordelia, dead back on Earth. A clean sweep — almost. The only person Jobs had left was his little brother, Edward. And Edward was only six. He was a responsibility more than anything else. Still, Jobs had to take care of him. If he lost Edward, he would be totally alone.

Maybe he'd fallen asleep because he was sad. Maybe he was just tired after battle. Either way, it was a stupid — possibly suicidal — thing to do. He was the one who had the best idea of how to sail this ship. Judging from the ship's wild motions, his little nap just might kill them all.

Jobs looked out at the water.

The waves didn't look especially dangerous. Especially not after the high winds and big sea of the storm that swallowed Billy, Mo'Steel, and Wylson. But the waves were big enough considering they were hitting the ship broadside.

Jobs carefully moved aft toward the helm. He found 2Face, Violet, Yago, and Edward clinging to the helm. As usual, 2Face and Yago were arguing with the intensity of siblings.

Violet, who liked to be called Miss Blake, was standing somewhat apart. Back on Earth, she'd belonged to a clique of girls called "Janes." They tried to re-create the world created by the author Jane Austen — a world of formality and femininity.

No sign of the others. No sign of the adults. This was the first environment the computer had created that allowed them to hide from one another, to spend some time alone. Olga, Mo'Steel's mother, was probably somewhere dealing with her own grief.

"We have to turn her," Jobs called. "Turn her to face the waves!"

"I thought of that!" Yago yelled. His face had an unnatural gray cast. "But we can't! The wheel's broken."

"Broken?" Jobs repeated, hanging on to the wheel to keep from sliding with the exaggerated motion of the ship. "No, that can't be right. The problem is that we have no momentum. The helm won't respond unless we're moving forward."

"We need to unfurl another sail," Edward said.

"Right," Jobs said.

Yago nodded sagely. "Before we unfurl another sail, we should take down the highest portion of the mainmast. They come in three pieces."

"What's that supposed to do?" Jobs asked.

"Lower our center of gravity," Yago said.

"Not much," Jobs said. "That section of the main-mast probably weighs five, six hundred pounds. That's nothing compared to the weight of the ship and the cannons."

"I've seen it done," Yago said.

"Yeah, but that must have been on a modern yacht with hydraulic lifts," Jobs argued. "All we have here are primitive ropes and pulleys. What if one of the ropes snaps? If we drop that thing, it will plunge right through the decks and possibly straight through the bottom of the ship. Oh, and here's another problem. Once we get it down, we'll never get it back up there again."

"It comes down," Yago said, covering his mouth with one hand and closing his eyes. His complexion had turned even grayer. It was almost unsettling to see the plastic-surgery poster boy look so unattractive.

"How?" Jobs demanded.

"Details aren't my thing," Yago snapped. "Work it out. Consider yourself my chief technical officer. Now, you'll have to excuse me. I need to — go belowdecks."

Yago staggered away, ending the discussion.

Jobs sighed and looked up into the rigging.

"Maybe that portion of the mast is heavier than I think."

2Face laughed bitterly. "Or maybe Yago is trying to get you killed! I don't think he likes it when someone corrects him."

Jobs didn't buy that. Except for cartoon-character villains, nobody was that ruthless. 2Face had an Oliver Stone complex. She was always imagining conspiracies. But Jobs was willing to cut her some slack. Her father, Shy Hwang, had died that day during the battle with the Blue Meanies. Slowly, they were all turning into orphans — he and Edward, Violet, 2Face.

"Tell us what to do," Violet said.

Jobs considered. Then, "Go belowdecks and round up Anamull, Roger Dodger — and, um, Tate, and D-Caf. Tell them I need them in the mainmast rigging, pronto. Ask Anamull to bring as many tools as he can carry. Screwdrivers, wrenches, pliers, and as much rope as he can find."

Violet started toward the ladder.

"You're actually going to take down part of the mast?" 2Face demanded. "Just because Yago said so?"

Jobs shrugged. "I've been sailing exactly twice in

my life. Once in a tourist boat around San Francisco Bay. Once in a Sunfish on a pond during Boy Scout camp. Yago has probably spent weeks floating around in presidential yachts. Why is it so hard to believe he knows something I don't?"

"Because he's an idiot," 2Face said without a hint of humor. "He thought the helm was broken!"

"Everyone makes mistakes," Jobs said.

"So you're going?"

"I'm going."

"I'll come," 2Face said angrily.

"Listen, if you don't want to —"

"I'm coming!"

"Fine. Whatever."

Jobs felt a little better as he led the way up the wet rope ladder, struggling to keep his footing as the swells tossed the ship. He couldn't think about Mo'Steel's death when he was fighting to prevent his own.

The first platform was the size of a living room and featured a wooden deck. Shy Hwang, who could cite all sorts of statistics about the ship once called the *Constitution,* had told Jobs this was called a fighting top.

Breathless, Jobs paused. This was his first climb into the rigging. From the deck, the height had looked terrifying. The reality was much, much worse. Jobs would have liked to sit and break down into great blubbering sobs, but he simply didn't have the time.

Jobs helped pull Tate up beside him. The deck was already more than a hundred feet below them.

"Keep going," Tate said. "If I stop now, I may never go any farther."

Tate had spent her time on the *Constitution* doing what she could to help belowdecks. Jobs knew she was scared. But he also knew he needed all the help he could get with the mast.

"Okay. Just try not to look down." Jobs started up toward the next platform. He kept his eyes on the ladder, doing his best to ignore their exaggerated side-to-side motion.

What if Tate or one of the others fell climbing up here? It would be Jobs's fault. What if Edward fell?

Don't think about that, Jobs told himself. *Just climb.*

He moved up the ladder, carefully avoiding the spots where Blue Meanie fire had torn holes.

Hand. Hand.

Foot. Foot.

Up and up.

And side to side to side. The higher they climbed, the more exaggerated the movement of the ship below them. They were climbing toward the end of the pendulum.

At the extreme edge of each roll, the deck below them disappeared and they hung out over the open ocean. Jobs imagined himself falling through the air and hitting the water. From this height, it would be as solid and bone-crushing as concrete.

It was dizzying, terrifying.

Jobs felt his shoulders tightening, knees weakening, heart pounding against his ribs. He had only one thought in his mind: *Mo'Steel would have loved this.*

CHAPTER THREE

"ONE, TWO, THREE — PULL!"

Jobs stood on the swaying upper fighting top and examined the mast construction. Or tried to. He was distracted by the height, by the ship's movement. It was hard to see in the moonlight. And the Blue Meanie fire had shredded some of the old pine masts.

Still, he was impressed.

Almost impressed enough to forget his fear.

This ship had been an exact replica of the one constructed before there were computers, hydraulic lifts, wind tunnels, or power tools. She'd been put together by a bunch of guys with saws and hammers and handmade nails.

And she was beautiful.

Jobs loved the simplicity of her construction. It was as elegant as an algebraic formula. So solid, so obvious, so straightforward. One good look was enough to tell him how it was built and why.

The mast sections overlapped for a good eight or ten feet. The lower section dead-ended into a wooden cap piece shaped like a squarish cough drop. The cap piece was approximately three feet square and supported the upper mast.

One by one, the others gathered until the platform was crowded. Everyone was clinging to the mast, the rope ladder, or one another and talking about how they could lift the mast — *if* they could do it.

"Can you see how it's put together?" 2Face called.

"The lower piece is jointed into this cap piece," Jobs said. "That's not going to move. I need to get higher to see how the top mast fits in."

Jobs climbed a few more feet up the rope ladder and looked down through the mess of rigging.

The upper mast sat in a round hole in the cap piece. It was held in place by a roller, cleats, nails, copper sheathing, and who knows what else. Their first job would be removing all that stuff. Then they were going to have to hoist the whole mast up the entire length of the doubling, attach ropes, and lower it to the deck without ruining the rigging. And they'd have to do it while the ship continued to roll wildly. The job required a lot of muscle power. And brains.

Woolly.

Shy Hwang said this ship had carried a crew of hundreds of men. Maybe hoisting the mast wouldn't have been too hard with twenty or thirty hands. Jobs had six.

Definitely woolly.

Ignoring his misgivings, Jobs got busy with the pliers, pulling out dozens of nails, cleats, and sheathing until the mast seemed to be loose in the cap. Tate helped him.

When they were finished, Jobs explained his plan to the others: Attach ropes to the upper mast section near the cap piece, get up above the mast on the rope ladder, and pull it up. Then retie the rope for better balance and lower the mast to the deck.

Nobody else had a better idea, so Jobs secured the rope and tossed one end to 2Face. "2Face, D-Caf, and Anamull, take this and climb the starboard ladder. Don't pull until I tell you."

"No," 2Face said.

"What do you mean no?" Jobs asked.

"I mean I'm not working with Yago's killers."

"I'm not a killer," Anamull said with a leer. "I'm a lover."

"You tried to feed me to the baby," 2Face said. "I'm *not* working with you."

"Tell you what," Jobs said. "Roger Dodger, why don't you work with D-Caf and Anamull? 2Face, you're with me, Tate, and Edward. Wait for my signal!"

They got into place. Jobs was farthest up on the ladder with 2Face and Edward in the middle and Tate closest to the platform.

"Everyone ready?" Jobs called. He couldn't see Anamull, Roger Dodger, and D-Caf from his position.

"Ready!"

"We go on three!"

Jobs waited until the ship reached a more or less vertical position. "One, two, three — pull!" he yelled.

Grasping the rope with one hand, Jobs pulled with the other. His grip on the rope slipped, snagging his skin, rubbing his hand raw. The mast didn't budge.

"Maybe we left a nail in there!" Tate yelled.

"I don't think so," Jobs yelled.

Another swell was rolling the ship toward port.

"Wait!" 2Face yelled. "Hold on until we get back on the vertical!"

Jobs clung to the rope ladder and watched the water grow closer and closer. If he'd wanted to, he could have reached out and touched it. Then, slowly, the ship began to right itself.

"Everyone still here?" Jobs called. "Okay, three, two, one — pull!"

This time, Jobs balanced with his feet and pulled with both hands. He gave it everything he had. His shoulder muscles strained and he felt something pop in his neck. He could hear 2Face and Tate grunting with effort.

Nothing.

Nothing.

Nothing — and then a high-pitched squeal and the mast lurched free.

"All right!" Jobs yelled.

But now they were rolling toward starboard. Rolling and rolling and rolling.

"Hold on!" someone cried.

Jobs saw the danger too late. With the mast section loose, swinging free, nothing was supporting it except the rope they were holding. The more the ship rolled, the more weight they had to support.

"I — I can't hold it!" Roger Dodger yelled.

"It's okay, kid, I got it!" Anamull yelled.

Another worry fought its way into Jobs's panicky brain. The free mast's weight was pulling them even farther to the starboard. The added weight just might be enough to upset the delicate balance that kept the entire ship from tipping over. Basic physics.

"Drop it!" Jobs yelled, immediately letting the rope slip out of his fingers. "Drop it, drop it, drop it! Now!"

The mast fell toward the water, their rope trailing after it. It hit the water without making a splash and sunk immediately.

Jobs clung to the ladder and watched as the water moved farther away. He was bathed in a cold sweat.

"Gee," 2Face said. "I'm glad we did that. That was really fun, wasn't it?"

(CHAPTER FOUR)

"THE MOST WE CAN DO IS OFFER A PRAYER."

Mo'Steel got up and started to yell. "Hello! Help! Whoever is out there, let us out of here!"

Billy Weir did not move. He could wait.

Billy felt dizzy, drunk with the sights and sounds flooding into his mind and with the reactions of his body — skin breaking out in a sweat and then cooling, heart beating faster and then more slowly, mind flitting from thought to thought like a kaleidoscope. Everything happening quickly, everything flowing together. No time to think, no time to sort real from unreal.

"Hang on!" came a voice from outside. An adult man, Billy thought. Not an American. His voice had too much music in it. "We're going to get you out."

The door opened off to one side and light flooded in.

Billy stayed in the shadows.

Mo'Steel leaped out of the door and then took a fast step back. "Whoa!" he said, shaking his head in surprise.

Two people were at the door. A man. And another person, an extraordinary person. A person who looked like an illustration from Billy's *Encyclopaedia Britannica*.

Billy remembered sitting on the floor of Big Bill and Jessica's bedroom and discovering the illustrations of MAN and WOMAN in the heavy, leather-bound p-book dating back to Jessica's own childhood.

The figures were covered with layers of transparent pages. Turn the first filmy page and you removed MAN's skin and exposed all that was underneath.

This person standing before Billy looked like that illustration brought to life. Wherever his clothes left his flesh visible, his skin was transparent. Arms, neck, face, scalp.

Billy saw the muscles in the monster's face tighten as he narrowed his eyes. Billy examined the veins running over and under the muscles like tree roots, the packets of yellowish fat in the monster's cheeks, the smooth grayish muscles sweeping from his forehead up over his scalp, the vulnerable pulsing of his fat jugular vein.

This monster had never appeared in any of his dreams.

Unless this was a dream.

He had seen things during the war in Chechnya. Dead soldiers, Chechen and Russian both. Shattered bleached white bones. Raw hamburger flesh. But nothing like this.

The monster saw Billy staring and gave him a hard look. His eyes were the green of late summer leaves. Burning. Undeniably human.

"I am Alberto DiSalvo and this — this is my son, Frederico." The man's voice was twisted with emotion. Not a good one. Pain? Fear?

"Kubrick," the monster said angrily.

"Hey, I remember you!" Mo'Steel said. He was talking to the man, but his eyes were drawn back to the monster over and over like a moth flitting toward a light. "I'm Mo'Steel. Remember? You were hitting the snooze button right around the time the worms showed up."

"I — I think I remember seeing you," Alberto said. "Then, then, we must have fallen asleep. When I woke up, we were in some sort of, um, laboratory."

Billy felt a shudder. Not in his body — in someone's mind. He caught a flash of something that could have been Alberto's memory or Kubrick's or both mixed. Nausea, a dusty machine cutting Kubrick's skin off in ridiculous small patches, anger, a sense of satisfaction.

Yes, Kubrick savored his father's anguish. His father had always treated him as if he were damaged — and now he was.

Or not.

Billy couldn't be sure. Couldn't tell if he was making this up, telling himself fairy tales.

He watched Alberto pull Mo'Steel a few feet away. "We have to find whoever or whatever did this to my son," he whispered. "Can you help us?"

"I thought you'd never ask," Mo'Steel said. "Let's go. Come on, Billy."

"What about Wylson?" Billy asked, speaking for the first time.

"Who's Wylson?" Alberto asked.

"A woman," Mo'Steel said. "One of us. She — she just died. Is there any place down here we could leave her? Maybe bury her?"

"No." Alberto stepped forward into the darkened room while his son hung back. He knelt down next to Wylson, took her pulse, and then pursed his lips. "Yes, she's dead. But we can't bury her. There isn't a proper place. The most we can do is offer a prayer."

Alberto stayed where he was, eyes closed, head bowed. Billy remembered the way he, Jessica, and Big Bill used to join hands and give thanks before meals in their huge tiled kitchen.

Billy felt a wave of sadness. The same sadness that had been with him for as long as he could remember.

Wylson was gone.

He'd thought he could save her.

(CHAPTER FIVE)

"GIVE THAT BOY THE CANNED HAM!"

Mo'Steel stepped away from the small room that had been his prison and did a slow 360-degree turn. He felt as if he were standing in the middle of Kansas. The space was vast.

Alberto and Kubrick were watching him closely, gauging his reaction. Billy hung back, either uneasy about stepping into the open or just lost in his own thoughts.

Here and there, Mo'Steel saw a massive metal I-beam column, but no walls were visible in any direction. The floor seemed to be made of metal covered with a gray-green coating like paint. The floor reminded Mo'Steel of a submarine hull.

But the ceiling was the interesting thing.

"If Guinness has a record for the universe's largest fish tank, this place has got to be in the book," Mo'Steel said.

"It's made of a substance similar to glass, only more perfectly transparent," Alberto said.

Mo'Steel stared up. The place reminded him of the Monterey Aquarium. He kept expecting a horn shark or a garibaldi to swim by overhead.

Not likely. Mo'Steel felt a strange pang as he remembered that Earth and all of the little fishies in its oceans were history. He wasn't about to get weepy over a bunch of flora and fauna, but he couldn't quite get used to the idea that Earth was totally and completely gone.

Mo'Steel noticed what looked like a block of white marble resting against the glass. He took a few steps in one direction and peered up at it, trying for a better view. "Look at that!" he said. "Billy? Is that what I think it is?"

"The base of a statue."

"Give that boy the canned ham! Look — there's another one over there," Mo'Steel said, pointing.

"So?" Alberto asked impatiently.

"So — we were up there, man! So were you, when you woke up on the ship. That's the ocean where we were sailing around in the *Constitution*. Those are the bases of the statues we were sailing around. I think we might be under *The Thinker* right now."

"The *Constitution*?" Alberto asked.

"Yes," Mo'Steel said, reminding himself that Kubrick and Alberto knew nothing of the weird environments they'd experienced and trying to slow down enough to bring them up to speed. Skipping many, many details, he told them about the Tower of Babel and the revolutionary warships the computer had created. "We're looking up at the world as we've known it," Mo'Steel finished.

"We're in hell," Kubrick said.

"No, we're in the basement," Mo'Steel said.

The place had a definite basement vibe. It was slightly musty, as if it hadn't been visited in a long, long time. It even gave him the run-up-the-stairs-to-safety basement creepies. Not so squirmy he couldn't handle it, but not good, either.

"I bet there's a wet bar and a pool table around here somewhere," Mo'Steel said. "Let's go check out one of those columns. Maybe we can find the stairs to the kitchen."

"You can't just go marching around down here," Alberto said harshly.

Mo'Steel sighed. Alberto was the kind of adult who was always ruining his fun. He looked like a panic attack waiting to happen. Eyes too jumpy, nerves too fried.

"Don't worry, I promise to be careful," Mo'Steel said. He headed toward the closest column, but Billy caught his hand. "That one," he said, pointing off to their right.

Mo'Steel didn't argue. Not with Billy. The dude had powers, freaky powers, and if he liked one column better than another, then fine.

Billy and Mo'Steel led the way. Alberto and Kubrick followed closely behind — so close Mo'Steel had the uncomfortable feeling they were going to step on the heels of his shoes.

Mo'Steel could guess what that meant. They were scared to walk across the open floor. They somehow knew or guessed that the floor was booby-trapped as thoroughly as a rice paddy in Cambodia or someplace. Mo'Steel pulled Billy into line behind him and continued.

Every step was dangerous.

Every step might trigger an explosion or something worse. Still, Mo'Steel didn't hesitate. He walked briskly, loving the risk, the uncertainty. He was almost disappointed when they got close enough to the column to see it better.

Mo'Steel was surprised to see that the column continued up into the environment above. He craned his neck, trying to get a better view. The statue was broad, solid, substantial. It lacked the rectangular base most of the statues they'd sailed past rested on. Even from down below, Mo'Steel could see the statue was old. He recognized the thing. He'd seen it during the last few minutes he'd spent aboard the *Constitution*.

"It's the Squid statue," he said.

Billy nodded wordlessly.

"Squids?" Alberto asked.

"When we got flushed, a battle was taking place around that statue," Mo'Steel said. "Looks like the fight is over now, though."

"Who was fighting?" Kubrick asked eagerly.

Mo'Steel studied him. He'd be useful in a battle. He was angry enough. Mo'Steel was getting used to Kubrick's see-through look, too. The shock was wearing off. Fake skin was only slightly more radical than fake bones and Mo'Steel had plenty of those.

"Aliens," Mo'Steel said. "Blue Meanies and Squids."

Kubrick and his dad exchanged looks, and Mo'Steel smiled. They thought he was crazy. Well, why not? They would see for themselves eventually. If they lived long enough.

"Why were they fighting over a statue?" Kubrick asked.

Mo'Steel shrugged. "Maybe they needed a focal point for their living room."

Alberto had a distant look in his eyes. The same look Jobs got when he was pondering a thorny puzzle. "You say this master computer creates environments based on the data we had aboard the shuttle?" Alberto asked.

"Best as we can figure," Mo'Steel said.

"And the other statues up there were recognizable masterpieces?" Alberto asked.

"We saw *David*," Mo'Steel said. "Something by Picasso. The Sphinx."

"Did anyone up there recognize this — this Squid statue?" Alberto asked.

"Don't think so," Mo'Steel said uncertainly. "Things were happening kind of fast. Not a lot of time for chitter chatter. Why? What are you getting at?"

"I don't think this is a statue," Alberto said. "The other statues are contained in the environment, as you call it. This is the only one that continues down into the basement. I think this is a part of the ship."

Alberto began to move around the column, studying it from every angle. Billy grazed it with his fingertips. Kubrick didn't seem to be doing more than staring off across the vast basement, putting as much space as possible between himself and his father.

Mo'Steel's mind had already moved on. He wanted to find a way back up into the environment. Anything at all could be going on up there and he wanted part of the action.

"What else is down here?" he asked Kubrick.

"Not much," Kubrick answered. "No way out that we could find. Rooms like the one you came out of. Some equipment, but we haven't been able to make any sense of it."

"What kind of equipment?" Mo'Steel asked.

"Computers."

"Show me," Mo'Steel said.

"I don't think that's a good idea," Kubrick said.

"Why? What are you guys so afraid of?"

"Those," Kubrick said, his gaze settling on something behind Mo'Steel.

CHAPTER SIX

"THE NEW WORLD IS A BIG MOVIE THEATER."

Mo'Steel spun around just in time to see massive pillars of brilliant light snap into existence. They were like three-foot-thick laser beams randomly spaced. Mo'Steel instantly imagined gigantic movie projectors projecting toward the ceiling.

"Grab your seats, everyone," Mo'Steel said. "Looks like the light show is just beginning."

The lights played against the glass ceiling, changing from blue to brown to white. Mo'Steel moved closer to get a better look.

Kubrick grabbed his arm and pulled him roughly back. "Careful," he said.

"What's the big deal?" Mo'Steel asked. "It's just light."

"So are laser beams, just light," Alberto said. "That doesn't stop them from cutting through bone. Watch this."

He yanked a button off the ragged jacket he wore. "See this button?" he asked like a magician. He waited for Mo'Steel to nod and then cautiously approached one of the light beams and tossed the button in.

"So?" Mo'Steel asked.

"Wait," Alberto said.

A few minutes passed, and then the lights clicked off as if someone had thrown a switch in the projection room. Mo'Steel stared at the floor around where the beam had been.

No button.

"The lights are extremely destructive," Alberto said. "Dissolving metal takes great quantities of energy."

"Also, they come up in different places each time," Kubrick said. "The only safe place is near the pits."

"Now that we know what's up there," Alberto said, "I think they must be some sort of matter-energy projectors creating the different environments."

"The New World is a big movie theater," Mo'Steel said. "And we got stuck in the projectionist's booth somehow."

"Something like that," Alberto agreed.

"So where are the controls?" Mo'Steel asked.

"Maybe we can get rid of the war scenes and play some extreme-skiing disks."

"Are you good with computers?" Alberto asked.

"Not especially," Mo'Steel said.

"Pity," Alberto said. "Still, you're right. We have at least fifteen minutes before the lights come back. Come on. I'll show you the pits. Those are as close to controls as anything we've found."

They started off across the vast open space with Alberto leading the way, suddenly brave and in control now that there was no immediate danger. He walked fast, then faster and faster until he was practically jogging.

Soon Mo'Steel could see where they were heading: a sunken pit that resembled a living room. The space glowed with a dim light. Fabric-covered chairs like the bucket seats in a fast car were spaced here and there, but Mo's attention was drawn to something that looked roughly equivalent to the plasma screen on his old computer at home.

He hopped down into the pit and eagerly tapped the screen with his fingertips. "Come on, baby," he muttered. "Give me something."

Nothing. He ran his fingers along the edges searching for a button. Nothing. There was no keyboard, no help button, no friendly talking interface. Nothing, zilch, nada, zero. Not even a dusty p-manual.

Where was Jobs when you needed him?

Oh, right, upstairs trying to sail a ship that had already been a relic when his grandmother was born.

Mo'Steel took a step back, frustrated, unable to think of what to do next. He bumped into Billy, who was hovering right behind him.

"Billy, sorry, man," Mo'Steel said. "I sort of forgot you were underfoot."

"It's a face," Billy said.

"A face?"

"It has no brain," Billy said.

"I think he's saying that it's a screen, a readout," Alberto said impatiently. "The brains of the machine are elsewhere."

"So let's look," Mo'Steel suggested.

For the next ten minutes, Alberto and Mo'Steel crawled around in the pit. They searched the panels, the chairs, and even the floor with their fingertips. Mo'Steel found nothing. Not even an old paper clip or a dusty piece of gum.

Billy and Kubrick sat on the floor. Not exactly together, just near each other. The two of them watched as the others searched.

"Dad, we've tried that a hundred times," Kubrick said finally.

"What do you suggest we do instead?" Alberto said.

"I don't know," Kubrick said. "I just know that what you're doing is pointless."

Angry red blotches broke out on Alberto's face and neck. "Fine," he said. "You think you're so smart, that's just fine. You figure out what we should do next."

"While you do what?" Kubrick demanded.

"Rest," Alberto said harshly. "I want to close my eyes on this godforsaken place and, if my brain will let me, actually forget I'm here for as long as I can sleep."

"You mean you want to get away from me," Kubrick muttered.

Alberto made no sign that he'd heard his son.

Mo'Steel watched with amazement as Alberto defiantly climbed onto one of the padded chairs. He had to work at it. The chairs hadn't been built for humans. They were too far off the ground. Alberto was forced to scramble up like a little kid. Once he was seated, the armrests hit him at about shoulder height.

"Do you think the Blue Greenies or the Squids built this stuff?" Kubrick asked. He seemed determined to ignore his father's little temper tantrum.

"Blue *Meanies*," Mo'Steel said. "And no. The proportions are all wrong. Check out the ergonomics. Whoever built that had long legs, short arms, and a huge head."

Mo'Steel watched as Alberto yawned, stretched, and settled himself into the alien chair.

"Can I get you anything?" Kubrick asked. "Maybe a pillow and your slip —" He trailed off when Alberto suddenly sat up.

"This thing is active!" Alberto exclaimed, all hints of anger or impatience gone from his voice. "I heard music. Very fast music. Oddly fast."

"Do you think it's the computer interface?" Mo'Steel asked eagerly.

"That's exactly what I think!" Alberto said.

"You guys haven't sat in one of these before?" Mo'Steel demanded.

"We have, several times," Alberto said. "But not this one. Maybe the others were inoperative." A broad smile lit up his face as he settled back in the chair. "There it is again!" he reported. The smile faded as he concentrated on what he was hearing.

"Music. Nothing I recognize. Getting faster now. More . . ."

His face blanked out. Like a TV screen does when you pull the plug. He was still looking at them, but his eyes were dead. His mouth dropped open so wide Mo'Steel could see a filling glittering in one of his molars.

Then his eyes rolled back in his head.

CHAPTER SEVEN

"THE CIVIL WAR IS ALREADY ON."

Jobs knew the others were tired and generally annoyed with life and one another.

He was tired and annoyed.

They'd struggled with the mast for hours. That was according to Jobs's internal clock. He didn't have a watch to consult and the night sky above them remained completely unchanged. No darkening into deep night like the real sky. A painter's version of reality.

His back hurt. Right in the middle. He tried to stretch it out, but that didn't seem to help.

Jobs thought that dropping the mast section had calmed the ship's swaying. A little. Maybe. Really, if Jobs was honest with himself, any effect was difficult to perceive. But he had a hard time believing they had done all that work for basically no reason.

"Now what?" Tate asked.

"Now we have to set the sail," Jobs said.

Six faces stared hostilely back at him. Jobs wondered if they were going to refuse. Then what? He'd have to try to do the job himself. They had to get control over the helm.

"Which sail?" 2Face asked finally. She sounded exhausted.

"I'll show you." Jobs didn't know the name for the sail, but he thought of it as the "main course" — a name he'd heard in some old movie about pirates. It was one of the biggest sails they had on board. It would be harder to set — much harder than the little sails they had been dealing with — but Jobs hoped it would be the only sail they'd need.

He led the way down the rope ladder to the next-lower platform. The others followed him, with Anamull reaching the platform last. The ship was still wallowing dangerously in the swell, but from the lower platform the movement seemed less extreme.

Just below them was the yardarm — a piece of wood that ran parallel to the mast like the short section of a cross. The sail was gathered up against the yardarm like a sail-sausage.

"We're going to have to climb down there to un-furl the sail," Jobs said. He pointed to a rope that ran about three feet below the yardarm.

Tate looked uncertain. "After you."

This was really more Mo'Steel's thing, Jobs thought as he headed down the ladder toward the yardarm. The thought made his heart feel even heavier.

Jobs climbed down until the yardarm was even with his waist. He reached out and placed his right foot on the foot rope. He gave it a little weight to test its strength. The rope sagged a little, but held.

The foot rope was maybe an inch in diameter. Several lengths of similar rope connected the foot rope to the yardarm. Jobs couldn't see what was holding the connector pieces in place — probably nothing more than a complicated knot.

Jobs sighed. The *Constitution* was beautiful and all, but he longed for steel and titanium and nylon. Materials that weren't weakened by things like sun and salt water. Materials you could trust.

"You going to stand there all night?" Tate had come down the ladder behind Jobs.

"No," Jobs said. "Just taking a moment to ponder my own mortality."

"Maybe it's better not to do that," Tate said.

Jobs nodded, moved his left arm onto the yardarm, stepped out onto the foot rope, and inched over to make room for Tate.

It was like walking a tightrope. A wet, slippery tightrope. He had a dizzying view of the deck hundreds of feet below. A view he did not enjoy.

Tate stepped onto the foot rope. Her added weight gave Jobs a good bounce. He felt his heart pounding in his throat as he clung to the yardarm. 2Face came after her.

"The rest of you need to go to port!" Jobs called. He didn't want anyone else on his side of the foot rope. It was bouncy enough already. One good bounce at the wrong time would land him in the ocean or toss him down onto the deck.

D-Caf, Anamull, Edward, and Roger Dodger moved into position.

The sail was attached to the yardarm with a series of short sections of rope. They spent ten minutes fighting to loosen the slippery wet knots. Jobs's fingers were bruised, raw, and bleeding before the job was half done. When they were finally finished, the sail loosened up on the yardarm. But it was still gathered up like a fancy window treatment.

"Let go of the lines!" Jobs called, pointing above his head.

Four lines lashed the sails in place. Jobs inched

over until he could reach one. The rope was curled around a wooden cleat. Jobs uncurled it and let it out. The far starboard side of the sail dropped down and began flailing in the wind.

"Roger Dodger! D-Caf!" Jobs yelled above the noise. "Get down on deck and tie the sail down."

"Aye-aye!" D-Caf said with one of his strange, nervous laughs.

Fifteen minutes and dozens of little adjustments later, the job was done. Violet turned the ship into the swells and Jobs had the satisfaction of feeling the ship calm under him.

Finally.

Jobs did a sidestepping walk back to the fighting top. His back and shoulder muscles ached, but he felt exhausted in a good way. All of the hard work had been worth it.

"Let's get something to drink," Tate said with an enormous yawn.

"What do you want?" Anamull asked. "Salty water or rum mixed with salty water?"

"Whatever's left," Tate said. She swung off the platform and began climbing down the rope ladder. Anamull was right behind her. Jobs was about to follow when he felt someone touch his arm.

2Face.

"Wait," she whispered urgently. "I need to talk to you."

Jobs sighed deeply. He was tired. He didn't feel like having a heavy conversation. On the other hand, 2Face had lost her father that day. He could spare her a few minutes. He stayed put while Anamull and D-Caf scuttled by them and made their way down the ladder. Anamull gave Jobs a long questioning look, but Jobs ignored him.

"What do you think of the situation?" 2Face asked when they were alone. She stood on the platform, hands resting lightly on the rail, gazing out to sea. The scene seemed a lot less threatening now that the ship had calmed.

Jobs rubbed his eyes with the heels of both hands. He took his time. When he finished, he rolled his head back and forth from side to side. "What situation?" he finally asked.

"Wylson washed overboard," 2Face said. "We have to presume she's dead. I don't know about you, but I'm wondering who that leaves in charge. Yago seems to think it's him."

"Why don't we just wait and see what happens?" Jobs asked wearily.

"We can't," 2Face insisted. "It's too dangerous. Listen, Jobs, this isn't some meaningless thing like who gets to be prom queen. Yago is dangerous. I'm scared of him. And I think you should be, too."

Jobs looked out over the water and wished he could just ignore 2Face. Popularity contests hadn't been his thing on Earth and he saw no reason to change his ways now. What good had Yago and 2Face's struggle done them so far? None. The way he saw things, Mother, the ship's computer, was the one in charge. The rest of them were just trying to save their skins.

"Yago is a jerk," Jobs said. "I'll give you that much. But I don't think he's *dangerous*."

"You're wrong," 2Face said. "Yago's game is to divide people into normals and freaks. If he takes charge, I'll be an outcast. So will Chameleon, your kid brother."

"Don't call him that," Jobs said.

"He asked me to call him that," 2Face argued.

"I know, but I don't like it," Jobs said.

"Fine. Whatever."

Edward had awakened on the shuttle with a new and disturbing ability: He could take on the characteristics of the environment surrounding him. It was like his own personal, built-in, adaptable camouflage. Jobs figured the mutation must have come about when Edward was exposed to radiation on their long voyage.

Jobs didn't feel like talking about Edward's strange mutation to anyone. Maybe, if they ignored it, it would just fade away in time.

2Face would never be so lucky. Her face — or rather half of her face — had been badly burned on Earth. The right side drooped and dripped like melted wax, pulling her eyelid down into a fixed expression of sadness. Nothing but a nub remained of her right ear. The effect of the damage was made even more startling by the perfection of the other side of her face.

"Don't worry about Edward," Jobs said. "He's my responsibility."

2Face let out an explosive sigh — obviously irritated by Jobs's reluctance to submit to her view of the world. "Look, I'm not living under Yago as boss."

"So what's the alternative?" Jobs asked, beginning to feel irritated himself. "You seem bent on starting some sort of civil war. Don't we have enough problems already?"

2Face took a deep breath. When she spoke again, her voice was calmer and quieter than it had been. "The civil war is already on. The question is who's going to win."

Coke versus Pepsi, Jobs thought. That's what this situation reminded him of. The cola giants were al-

ways trying to make you believe that the choice between their products was vital to your happiness.
But, when you came right down to it, what was the
difference? They were both peddling sugar water in
cans.

"I'll think about it," Jobs said as diplomatically as
possible. He began to move toward the top of the
ladder.

2Face put out a hand to stop him. "You don't
trust me, do you?" she asked.

Jobs stared at her arm, feeling defeated. He considered pushing by her, but what would be the
point? She'd keep after him until he agreed to join
her anti-Yago campaign or flatly refused to do so.

"I'd like to trust you," Jobs said. "But I know
you're not exactly an angel. Edward told me what
happened with the baby. The whole story," he added
with special emphasis.

Jobs hadn't wanted to believe it when Edward
took him aside and whispered his terrifying tale. He
hadn't wanted to believe that 2Face would sacrifice
Wylson to save herself. He hadn't wanted to believe
Tamara had demanded a sacrifice or that the others
had considered it. Sometimes he thought this place
was designed to test them, to see how depraved
they could become.

2Face fell quiet. Silence stretched out between them. Jobs wondered if the conversation was over, if he could just slip away now. But 2Face hadn't moved her hand.

"I'm not proud of that," 2Face said at last. "I regret it constantly. But, let me ask you this, would you submit to a terrible death to save — not someone you loved — but someone like Wylson?"

"I don't know," Jobs admitted.

"Well, until you do, maybe you shouldn't be so fast to judge me," 2Face said.

"I'm not judging you," Jobs said with effort. "I'm just saying . . . I'm saying the choice between you and Yago doesn't strike me as a choice between good and evil. Both choices suck for different reasons."

2Face didn't laugh. She didn't even smile. "I think I understand," she said. "You're like my father, like my father was. You're a coward. You don't want to choose because you're terrified of making the wrong choice. You're afraid someone will blame you if things go wrong. Of course, nobody can blame you if you refuse to get involved."

That hurt. Jobs stood there, without words, wondering if 2Face was right.

"You don't like me, that's fine, Jobs," 2Face said.

"But just remember it comes down to Yago, dividing people up into freaks and normals, or me. When the time comes, you'd better be ready to choose."

2Face pushed by him and started down the ladder.

Jobs stared out to sea, feeling completely lost. Ten minutes earlier, he'd thought 2Face was the closest thing he had left to a friend. Who did he have to turn to now?

CHAPTER EIGHT

"NOBODY ASKED HER TO GET ALL HEROIC . . ."

The hammock was a joke. It was made of some sort of itchy rope tied into knots that bit into Yago's back. He thought with longing of his bedroom suite back in the White House. Almost a thousand square feet all to himself, including a huge bed with a down mattress cover. Heaven. Pampering appropriate for the president's son.

Of course, his efforts to sleep weren't aided any by the total lack of privacy.

Olga was lying in the next hammock over. She'd been quiet and withdrawn ever since Mo'Steel went overboard. Yago wished she'd get a grip. Now was not the time for selfish concerns like grief.

Burroway had one of the hammocks, too. He wasn't sleeping. Apparently the motion of the ship was getting to him. He'd spent half the night moaning and gagging. At least Yago's own nausea had abated. Simple mind over matter. Burroway could learn a few things from him.

T.R. was down there somewhere, too, although Yago couldn't see far enough in the gloom to know what he was doing.

Yago did know one thing, however. Someone in the room was sporting some serious BO or passing some outrageous gas. He sighed. Just one more of the many irritations he'd had to deal with lately. Good thing he wasn't some spoiled brat who couldn't take it.

Between the swaying ship and the BO, sleeping was out of the question. Some fresh air would be nice, but Yago didn't want to risk going on deck until Jobs got the ship's swaying under control. Yago had zero desire to fall overboard. What would happen to these clueless people if he wasn't around to tell them what to do?

As usual when he couldn't sleep, Yago counted loyal supporters. Unfortunately, the exercise didn't take long.

D-Caf.

Period.

Maybe Anamull, although he was so silent and brutish who knew what he was thinking?

The adults — T.R., Olga, Burroway? A shrink, a

research scientist, and an astrophysicist. Not one of them was leadership material. Of course, that didn't mean they would follow Yago.

Tate. She'd probably go to 2Face. She'd stood up for 2Face when the baby was ready to have her for dinner.

Violet. Miss Blake. The Jane. *Mine,* Yago thought with pleasure. She always treated him . . . delicately. Like she respected him. Too bad about her finger. Deformities like that turned Yago's stomach. But it was the Jane's own fault. Nobody asked her to get all heroic and try to save Big Bill's life.

Roger Dodger. Too young to have a clue.

Ditto Edward. He'd do whatever Jobs told him. And what about Jobs?

Yago had not liked the way Jobs corrected him about the helm. Disrespectful. That was the only way to describe it.

On the other hand, Jobs did have the sort of geeky intelligence that could be useful in this nuthouse. Maybe it was time to get over their little disagreements and make nice-nice. With Mo'Steel gone, Jobs would be yearning for a friendly face. Yes, Yago could definitely take advantage of Mo'Steel's death where Jobs was concerned.

And what about Tamara and the baby? Now

there was a regular riddle wrapped in a mystery inside an enigma rolled up in a conundrum. Just thinking about Tamara and her flesh-eating spawn was enough to give Yago a headache.

Yago sighed. He had so much work to do. He had to work on Jobs, figure out how to get Tamara and the baby under his control, think of a way to make 2Face look bad.

One thing was certain: Battles were dangerous. The last one almost killed them. Forget the Blue Meanies. Forget the Squids. Forget the Riders. Let the three of them battle one another. The thing was to pick a direction and just keep sailing that way until they hit another node.

Yago would figure out how to conquer the aliens eventually. For now, he had his hands full just trying to conquer the humans.

CHAPTER NINE

"HAPPY PEOPLE DON'T MAKE NOISES LIKE THAT."

Kubrick snapped out of it first. He scrambled up and pulled his father out of the alien chair or computer interface or whatever it was. He expected resistance, some sort of force holding him in, but his father came out of the chair easily.

They landed on the floor on all fours. Kubrick immediately crawled out from under his father, but Alberto just laid there looking like a bug zapped by a bug zapper.

"Is he dead?" Mo'Steel asked.

"You check," Kubrick said, out of breath from exertion and fear.

Mo'Steel reluctantly got down on his hands and knees and slowly crawled closer. By that time, Alberto had begun to twitch and wail.

"Definitely alive," Mo'Steel said.

"What's wrong with him?" Kubrick demanded.

"Don't know," Mo'Steel said. "But whatever it is, it's woolly. Happy people don't make noises like that."

Alberto pushed Mo'Steel away. "2390.00026.13," he mumbled as he struggled to his knees and wiped the drool off his chin. "Self-diagnostic. No errors found."

"Well, that's a relief," Mo'Steel said. "Although I think you may want to run that program again."

"Dad, are you okay?" Kubrick asked, forcing himself to approach his father and touch his shoulder. "Papa? Papa, can you hear me?"

Alberto grabbed Kubrick's arm and pulled himself up to his knees and then his feet. He leaned heavily on Kubrick's shoulder. "Too much sad."

"Okay, this is weird stuff," Mo'Steel said. "Remind me never to take a nap around here."

Kubrick pushed his father away, grabbed his shoulders, and shook him. Hard. "Snap out of it!" he demanded. "Tell us what happened!"

Alberto wobbled and then steadied himself. Mo'Steel came forward and helped hold him up. Billy was nearby, too. Observing, but not getting involved.

Kubrick wished Billy would keep his distance.

Billy gave him the creeps. He was too pale, too spaced out, and yet too aware.

Disturbing.

Kubrick stared intently into his father's face and he thought he saw his eyes focus. "Tell us what happened!" he demanded.

Alberto licked his lips with a bloody tongue. Blood was also oozing out of his ears, nose, and the corners of his bloodshot eyes. He spoke with agonizing slowness. "It — an interface — computer. A control? Data. Too data, too sad. *Pazzo.*"

"*Pazzo?*" Mo'Steel demanded.

"Means crazy," Kubrick said.

"Does he mean he's crazy or the computer is crazy?" Mo'Steel asked.

"I don't know!" Kubrick exploded. "How should I know?! Listen, let's get something straight. Back on Earth, I wasn't exactly known for my high IQ. I definitely wasn't Ivy League material, get it? So don't keep coming to me with your questions."

"Whoa — relax," Mo'Steel said. "I'm more a man of action myself."

Kubrick got the horrible feeling he was going to cry, and it ticked him off. He was mad — at his father, and at himself for turning into freaky see-through boy. It was stupid, but he'd actually been looking forward to leaving bad old Earth behind and starting over in the New World. It seemed like the solution to all of his problems.

But things weren't turning out exactly how he'd expected. He couldn't deal with this weirdness. Couldn't deal with a computer attacking his father or stealing his skin. This wasn't what he had in mind. He wanted out, wanted to escape.

He wished he'd waited for the Rock back on Earth. Then he wouldn't have to worry about Mo'Steel checking out his new "look." He wouldn't have to worry about his father.

"Sit down, Papa," Kubrick said. "Sit down and rest awhile."

They climbed out of the pit and settled Alberto on the edge, hoping they were still close enough to the instruments to be safe from the light columns.

Billy stayed close to Alberto. Not touching him or commenting on his condition, just sitting. Watching? Kubrick couldn't tell but he didn't like it.

Alberto didn't improve. If anything, his twitching and jerking got more frequent and violent. He stared wildly and erupted into sudden torrents of disjointed words. Occasionally, he got stuck, repeating "gone" a few thousand times before lapsing into silence. Kubrick tried to make sense of what he was saying, but it was all a mad, unsettling jumble.

Pazzo.

That's what Alberto had said.

Kubrick was pretty sure he wasn't talking about the computer.

(CHAPTER TEN)

"IT'S TRYING TO KILL US."

When Yago woke, the other hammocks were empty. The sun was up and a weak light was coming through the portholes. The ship's movements had calmed. He could hear commotion on the deck.

Something was wrong.

Yago fought his way out of the hammock and climbed the ladder to the deck.

Everyone was up there. They were bunched together in twos or threes, talking tensely. Adults in one group. Tate, Edward, and Roger Dodger in another. Tamara and the baby, alone as usual. What the hell was going on? Why hadn't someone called him?

Just what he needed. A crisis before breakfast.

Yago noticed 2Face, Jobs, and Violet standing together just in front of the foremast. They looked tense. Yago felt his blood go cold. It was like seeing the chief of staff, majority whip, and vice president huddling in the West Wing. What were they doing? Planning a coup?

What would Mom do in a situation like this? Yago wondered. The answer came back immediately: Act cheery, unthreatened. Yes, cheery was definitely the thing.

"Good morning!" Yago said, joining the group. "Jobs, I'd like you to head this ship south."

Jobs stared at him. "South? We can't go south."

"South, north, I don't care," Yago said. "The point is to pick a direction and keep going that way until we reach the end of this environment, this node. Go whichever way the wind is blowing."

"Would you stop being such a pompous creep and look around you?" 2Face snapped.

Yago looked out at the ocean. The statues were gone, that was the first thing he noticed. And the water was calmer, much calmer. Also, there were more ships this morning.

2Face shook her head impatiently. "See those ships? Notice anything important about them? I'll give you a hint: Look at the flags."

"British," Yago said immediately.

"Very good," 2Face said. "And we're flying the American flag. Don't you think that just might make them a little bit angry?"

"So we take the flag down," Yago said with a shrug. "D-Caf! Do me a favor and take down those flags."

D-Caf immediately began climbing the mainmast in a way Yago found most gratifying.

"Good idea," Jobs said. "And let's find a white one to put in its place. Surrendering worked with the Squids. Let's try it again."

"Good idea," Yago said, smiling ingratiatingly at Jobs. He hated to do it, but he reminded himself that Jobs could be useful. "Edward! See if you can find some white fabric we can run up the flagpole."

Edward cast a questioning look at Jobs, who nodded. As soon as he received confirmation from his brother, Edward scurried belowdecks. Hmm. Yago didn't like that. He'd have to teach Edward where his loyalty should lie.

Yago studied the other ships more carefully. There were three of them altogether. The ships themselves were rather jaunty — painted gold and navy blue — much nicer than the *Constitution's* black and white, in Yago's opinion. Each one had four separate gun decks with cannons poking out under little trapdoors.

Swarms of men were climbing all over the rigging. They were close enough that Yago could make out individual men. Some wore white pants, navy jackets with gold trim, and hats. Officers. Others had on tan pants, striped shirts, and seemed to be barefoot. Crewmen.

"This is a new painting," Violet said thoughtfully.

"How do you know?" Jobs asked.

"The sky," Violet said. "Yesterday, the brushstrokes were smooth, almost invisible. This style is more impressionistic. I suspect whoever painted this scene didn't live during the Civil War era."

"Give me one reason why I should care," 2Face said.

Yago cringed. Next to Violet, 2Face seemed so brusque.

"Artists who were contemporaries of these ships had many reasons to paint them," Violet explained patiently. "Perhaps a crewman was interested in purchasing a painting of his ship to send home to his family. His only options were oils or watercolors. Later artists, however, were more likely to paint important moments in history. I believe battle scenes were particularly popular."

Yago found it difficult to follow Violet's little art history lessons. But Jobs seemed to be tracking. He nodded and looked glum. "You're saying painters aren't big fans of peaceful surrenders."

"Correct," Violet said. "Perhaps my observation is of no consequence. We can hope Mother will allow us to influence this environment in any way we wish. However, I think it's more likely that our surrender will result in the crewmen from the other ships boarding us and taking control with violence."

"It's trying to kill us," Yago blurted out. "Mother, the ship, the computer — whatever you want to call it — it wants us dead."

Jobs was shaking his head in his irritating know-it-all way. "If the ship wanted us dead, we'd be dead. I mean, think about it. We're lost, we have no weapons, we can't fly like the Meanies can."

"Sitting ducks," Yago said.

Jobs nodded. "Believe it or not, I think Mother is trying to create environments that we'll like."

Yago snorted. "Any more of this motherly love and we'll be loved to death."

2Face was gazing out at the British ships. "They're signaling one another," she reported. "I think they may be using mirrors."

"Probably getting ready to attack," Violet said.

Edward came back on deck. "Jobs, I can't find anything white anywhere," he reported.

Violet tore angrily at her shirt, ripping off one of

the sleeves just above the elbow. "This was white back on Earth. Maybe it will do."

Yago snatched the piece of cloth and handed it to Edward. "Get this to Anamull. Tell him to rig it up on the flagpole. Jobs, get the cannons loaded. Don't fire until I tell you to. Violet, see if you can maneuver out of striking range."

"How?" Violet asked. "We're surrounded."

Yago pointed toward two ships. One was at twelve o'clock, the other at three o'clock. "Straight through there," he demanded.

Jobs had started to go belowdecks, but now he hesitated. "Be sure not to turn our back to them," he told Violet. "We can't fire to the rear. No gun ports to the aft."

Yago felt his anger flare. He snapped his fingers in Jobs's face and pointed belowdecks. "Cannons! Now."

Jobs stared at him for a second, then turned and went.

Disrespectful, Yago thought. He'd have to do something about Jobs just as soon as this battle was over. But, for now, he needed him.

Jobs motioned to some of the others, and they all headed belowdecks. Arming the cannons was not a one-person job. At least, Yago didn't think it was. Actually, he had no idea how it was done.

He wasn't a detail guy.

Suddenly there was a terrific noise, followed closely by another and then another. Yago spun around in confusion. What was that? Where had it come from?

"Hey — they're firing at us!" 2Face yelled.

Already? That was crazy. He hadn't had time to think, to plan.

2Face pointed.

Billows of black smoke. The ship at twelve o'clock was surrounded by billows of black smoke. Cannonballs! Half a dozen heading directly for the side of the ship. Yago stood near the helm, staring stupidly, not knowing what to do.

Plop! Plop! Several cannonballs landed in the ocean. Short! Another hit the side of the ship and bounced off. Yes! But others ripped through the rigging and tore through the one sail they had set.

Debris rained down on Yago's head. Splinters, dust, god knows what. Yago held his hands over his head.

A high-pitched scream. Edward and Anamull came down the ladder, half falling in their eagerness. "We set the flag."

Great. It didn't seem to be doing much good.

Couldn't think. No time. The cannons wouldn't be ready to fire for ten, twenty minutes. Maybe longer. So they couldn't fight. Without sails, they couldn't even run away. Noise. Smoke. People shouting. Couldn't think.

Tamara! She was the only weapon they had. "Get me Tamara!" Yago yelled. "Go!"

Tate took off, heading toward the bow.

Incoming cannons arced overhead, followed by the pitter-patter of rigging and debris hitting the deck.

Then Tamara Hoyle was by his side, her creepy baby supported on one hip. The baby looked at Yago with eyes that were nothing but empty craters and grinned at him, exposing a mouth full of teeth.

Asking favors of the baby was dicey business. He knew there would be a price to be paid. *Think about that later,* Yago told himself.

"They're firing again!"

"Can you help?" Yago asked.

For a moment, Tamara looked distant, unfocused. Then, "No, not yet. If the other ships try to board us, yes. But not like this, not at a distance."

"Fine, okay," Yago said. "Get belowdecks. Get everyone belowdecks."

Tamara didn't seem worried. She turned, almost leisurely, and walked toward the ladder. Completely ignored another volley of incoming cannonballs. Combat training or something else? She was as calm as a lioness.

Yago heard a slow thundering sound, like a tree falling. He looked up in time to see the mainmast creak slowly to starboard, pulling loose a mass of rigging. The mast steadied for a moment, then picked up speed and started to fall faster. Yago halfrose and began to duckwalk out of the way. *Got to get be-lowdecks. Much safer belowdecks.*

With an enormous crash, the mast smashed into the deck, bringing down a section of the wooden wall that half protected them from the cannonballs. Yago was knocked onto all fours. He felt a distant flash of pain as his head whacked onto the deck.

CHAPTER ELEVEN

"THE COMPUTER IS MAD."

"And, and, and, and . . ." Alberto said. He was stuck again.

They'd been resting and listening to Alberto babble for what felt like a very long time. He was getting worse. He was beginning to remind Billy of the men who had cracked during the war. The ones who stumbled aimlessly around the village square, hearing explosions in their heads.

"And, and, and, and . . ."

"*And* let's get moving," Mo'Steel said, leaping to his feet. "We need to find a way upstairs."

Kubrick and Billy slowly got up, and Kubrick helped Alberto to his feet.

"Which way?" Mo'Steel asked.

Billy stayed silent.

Kubrick shrugged sullenly.

"Where are they?!" Alberto screamed wildly. "Today, tomorrow, next, next, on, on, and . . ."

Mo'Steel hesitated. Billy could feel his pain, his indecision. Then, a steadying. "Okay, follow me," Mo'Steel said. He picked a direction at random and started walking.

Billy followed Mo'Steel across the basement.

After being still for so long, walking felt strange and dangerous! Balancing on one foot while reaching ahead with the other. Balancing, then almost falling, until you caught yourself with the other foot and started over again —

"There's nobody to play with me!" Alberto shrieked suddenly. "Where is everyone? Where is my party invitation? I like birthday cake. I like pin the tail on the donkey. I can play charades and spin the bottle and two minutes in the closet. I could serve the tea and biscotti. Why wasn't I invited? Drifting!"

"Dad, cool it," Kubrick said harshly. He had been holding his father up, but now he shrugged off his arm angrily.

"Drifting . . ." Alberto whispered. "Lost, so lost. Mommy, I'm bored!"

"Dad!" Kubrick shouted.

"Ignore him, 'migo," Mo'Steel said. "The computer sent him on a bad trip. Give him some time to turn the car around and come home."

"Alone," Alberto said matter-of-factly.

Alone.

Billy's mind played with the word, turning it around and examining it from all angles. It was one of his favorite words. One of the words that had been his companion during five hundred years of silent awareness.

Lots of Alberto's words were old friends.

Pazzo. That was just "mad" twisted into another shape, dressed up for a holiday in Tuscany.

Lost.

Bored.

Drifting.

Why?

More old friends. If Billy were the type of crazy to drool and shout, these might be the very words he would shout between drooling spells. Sounded as if Alberto had a painful life.

Then a new thought occurred to Billy. He loved new thoughts! Loved feeling his brain close around something that wasn't there before. The existence of the thought was just as interesting as the thought itself.

Billy thought: *How did he know those were Alberto's words just because they came out of his mouth?* Other people's memories came into Billy's mind. Maybe Alberto was repeating what he had heard while he was connected to Mother's computer.

That would mean *why* and *alone* were the computer's words.

Pazzo was the computer's word.

The Meanies thought Mother was confused.

Maybe she was actually mad.

Computers are built to process information. Maybe the lack of new input could drive a smart-enough computer insane. The same programs running countless times. The endless repeating of dull binary code. Ones and zeros in perfectly predictable order, falling flawlessly into place over and over again.

Tedium could have pushed the computer over the edge.

Loneliness could have inspired her to pluck their shuttle out of space.

And then what? Did the computer like her new plaything? Were the humans a cure for her insanity — or just another trigger?

Could the computer, like Billy, find it hard to tell reality from unreality now that the world was unpredictable, changing, ebbing, out of control?

"I hear noises!" Mo'Steel announced. "Come on — this way!" He adjusted his course slightly and marched on, never wavering.

Mo'Steel can't be real, Billy thought. *A real person would be afraid of the laser lights of death.* Billy would have been afraid of them if he was real.

Billy wanted to ask Mo'Steel if they were hearing the same noises — something like distant thunder. But what was the point in talking to a figment of your imagination?

The others followed Mo'Steel. Alberto stumbled like a drunk, occasionally falling to his hands and knees and then picking himself up again. Kubrick helped him when he took too long.

"Freeze!" Mo'Steel shouted.

Billy started to take another step, but Mo'Steel grabbed him and pulled him down. Behind them, Alberto and Kubrick also hit the deck. The four of them cowered as the lights clicked on around them.

"This makes no sense," Mo'Steel said, staring up at the environment. "How can the world being created up there look constant when the lights turn on and off?"

"Nothing here makes any sense," Kubrick said bitterly.

Mo'Steel got to his feet. "Let's keep going. It's actually safer with the lights on. We can make some time while we know where to step."

"Wait," Kubrick said.

Mo'Steel and Billy turned and saw that Alberto was down. They doubled back. Alberto's head was hanging between his hands. He was ranting. "*Vuoto!* The desert, salt flats, wasteland, hinterland, Mother's basement, *deserto*, the face of the moon, outback, boonies . . ."

"Let me guess," Mo'Steel said. "Things that are empty."

"He sounds like a thesaurus," Kubrick said.

"Frontier," Alberto said. "Empty, all *vuoto*."

"What is he talking about?" Kubrick demanded.

"He isn't talking," Billy said. "He is repeating what the computer told him. The computer is crazy."

"How can a machine go crazy?" Mo'Steel asked.

"Very, very slowly," Billy said.

By the time they got Alberto up and moving again, Mo'Steel was in one sorry mood. Grumpy, impatient, ticked off. He'd had more than enough of walking across this dull plain of a basement. He wanted to do something normal — like board the *Constitution* and make like a rigging rat.

If only he could find some way up! He was about

ready to try clicking his heels together and saying, "There's no place like home."

The distant sounds were the only clue he had, so he doggedly headed toward them. Or tried. They seemed to move in random patterns. And, of course, it was hard to hear over Alberto's blabbering.

God, why were Yago and 2Face always fighting over who got to lead? Leading was for chumps. Zero fun.

As Mo'Steel trudged along, he took notice of the fact that the ceiling was getting lower. He could almost reach out and brush it with his fingers. Did that mean they were closer to the perimeter of the basement? And, if they were — who cared?

Jobs would probably have found some cosmic meaning in a low ceiling and suddenly located the up escalator. To Mo'Steel, all it meant was less headroom.

Then, suddenly, like an answered prayer, the sounds were closer. And then right overhead! Mo'Steel stopped to listen. Billy stopped just behind him, his eyes unfocused, mind disconnected. Kubrick stood a bit farther back, watching Mo'Steel warily. Alberto was wheeling, barely staying on his feet.

"Wake up, Billy Boy!" Mo'Steel shouted. "I think we found our ship!"

Mo'Steel felt like laughing as he looked up and saw a wooden keel scraping by just inches out of reach. His elation lasted long enough for him to breathe in, breathe out. Then he realized: The ship was right above him, but so what? That didn't get him any closer to getting on board. And, as he watched furiously, the keel started to move away. It was moving faster than he would have expected. The wind must really be whipping up there.

Kubrick started to shout. But that was stupid. What good would that do? They couldn't hear him up there, and even if they could, what would they do about it?

They had to follow the ship! Mo'Steel realized. That was it. That way they'd know where it was when they finally figured out how to get on board.

"Come on!" Mo'Steel shouted, starting to run.

"Watch it!" Kubrick yelled.

Mo'Steel had his eyes on the keel, up overhead. Kubrick's words registered a second too late. Mo'Steel shifted his gaze — but not in time to save himself, just in time to see the disaster ahead. A laser beam. Bright red. Right in front of him!

He jerked back, trying to cancel his momentum, trying to slow down before the light zapped him into nothingness.

Too late.

It was like walking out of a dark movie theater into the brilliant sunlight. Only this sunlight was red. The color of blood. The color of death.

Kubrick crouched, with Alberto blabbering at his side and Billy off in la-la land, and watched Mo'Steel disappear into the red beam. He could have rushed forward, could have tried to grab him, save him. There wasn't enough time, he didn't have a chance — but he could have tried.

He didn't. He just watched.

He wondered what Mo'Steel experienced. One last moment of excitement, one last rush — and then nothingness, release.

Mo'Steel had found a way out.

CHAPTER TWELVE

"BUT UP THERE, I'M BIG!"

Dying was a rush.

An adrenaline-powered ride. Caught up in the red beam, Mo'Steel felt electrified. His brain was switched on, hardwired to the power grid.

He was instantly and intensely aware of every cell in his body. It was like watching a billion different plasma screens simultaneously. He could see every one of his own cells like illustrations in a bio data chip. Jangles of nerve cells like twisted tree roots. Long, skinny muscle cells. Millions of boring block-like skin cells. Delicate brain cells pulsating with energy and looking like some fem's drawing of a snowflake. Solid, strong-looking molecules that had to be the titanium in the bones he'd had replaced.

Then, as he watched, the cells began to twitch, cytoplasm shaking like jelly, nuclei pulsating with energy. The cell membranes came unstuck and the cells moved away from one another like magnets with opposite poles.

Then — *POOF! POOF! POOF!* — a million silent explosions as each cell divided into billions of infinitely smaller atoms.

It didn't hurt. All Mo'Steel felt was a strange, almost pleasant sense of lightening and expanding. He wasn't scared. Why fear death? He couldn't bunny out even if he wanted to.

The atoms began to move. Sorting, separating, translating themselves. And now, Mo'Steel felt his tiny blasted-apart parts moving along the light beam itself like motes of dust.

Up, up, and up!

"Aaaahh!" Mo'Steel yelled in his soul, in his consciousness, because his mouth, brain, and lungs were scattered everywhere.

He sensed some sort of barrier and moved through it in all of his ridiculously tiny pieces.

Then, to Mo'Steel's surprise, the process began to reverse itself. Atoms unsorted and recombined to form cells. Cells moved closer and clung together.

He had a mouth.

He had a brain, ears, eyes.

Mo'Steel took a deep breath and looked down. He was amazed to see what looked like his own familiar chest slowly rising up out of a vast pool of water. And he was still growing. Up and up, like an educational data chip that showed two years of a plant's growth in two minutes.

He was still wearing the same tattered clothes, but as his arms emerged from the water, he saw sails attached under them like webs on a duck's feet.

Messed up.

Whacked.

But very, very interesting.

Now he noticed toy boats floating in the water. They were firing at one another. Mo'Steel could hear a tiny, tinny ping every time one of their guns fired. Little figures on the deck of each boat were staring up at him. Whoa — it was the *Constitution*! And Mo'Steel was pretty sure that skinny-looking action figure hugging the deck was Jobs.

Jobs was on the gun deck, looking out at the water. British cannonballs had punched big holes in the side of the ship.

Six of the *Constitution*'s cannons were loaded and ready to go. Olga and Burroway had handled the gunpowder and cartridges. D-Caf, 2Face, Anamull, Burroway, and Jobs worked up a sweat pulling the cannons out far enough to load them and securing them until they were ready to fire. Edward and Roger Dodger were also hanging around, attracted by the massive guns.

The British ships were drawing closer. Jobs admired the elegance of their movements, the way their captains set and furled sails with the help of dozens of crewmen. The ships moved purposefully. Another ten minutes and they would be close enough to board the *Constitution.*

Funny. This would be only the second battle the old frigate had ever lost. The other had been the day before against the Blue Meanies.

The *Constitution* — named after a then-just-drafted document that defined a fragile new democracy, the document that governed one of the most powerful nations Earth had ever seen. The *Constitution* — a proud American icon humbled by this ship's computer and their little band of Remnants.

Jobs wished he could be on the real *Constitution* fighting for freedom instead of in this crazed computer-generated environment where there was no honor, only survival.

"I say we shoot," Burroway said. "What's the point of going down with ammo still on board? Maybe we'll get lucky."

"Let's shoot," Edward pleaded.

Jobs shrugged. One of the other ships was so close it would be practically impossible to miss. They should shoot. Why not? Well, Jobs could think of some reasons. Like the danger of playing with matches — not to mention gunpowder and a weapon that weighed a thousand pounds, give or take a few hundred.

They'd figured out how to fire the big guns during the battle the day before. Jobs had called on a 507-year-old memory of a Civil War reenactment he'd seen on a field trip. Firing the cannons took teamwork, caution, and backbreaking work. It also took guts — because if you were lazy or unlucky or standing in the wrong place at the wrong time, you could lose a finger or your life.

"Release the cannon!" Jobs called tensely.

Edward scrambled forward and yanked free the blocks of wood that stopped the cannon from rolling around the deck. Olga pulled out the wooden plug that kept moisture out of the barrel.

"Move her into place!"

Anamull, T.R., Jobs, D-Caf, 2Face, and Olga hauled on the ropes that encircled the cannon's platform. Creaking and groaning, the wheels turned and the cannon moved forward until its barrel poked out through the gun port. Jobs crouched down and sighted along the barrel, but he immediately stood up. The British ship was right there. They couldn't miss.

"Fire!" Jobs yelled, stepping off to one side and taking a second to make sure Edward was clear.

Burroway touched a slow match to the touchhole in the top of the barrel.

A pause. Then —

Light flashed. A sulfurous smell filled Jobs's nose and his ears rang with a sound like thunder.

The cannonball raced across the space between the two ships, hitting the cartoon seamen about shoulder height. It made the ship balloon.

Wait. That didn't make sense. Cannonballs couldn't do that. Jobs blinked. Looked again.

The ship was rising up out of the water! It looked as if some gigantic animal was pushing up under it. Jobs thought of a whale, then of the blimp creatures that lived in the copper-colored sea that was the ship's default environment. It wasn't either of those things. This creature was covered with something that looked like brown cord.

"It's Mo'Steel!" Edward yelled.

Actually, it was Mo'Steel's head. Mo'Steel's head in a close-up big enough to fill a screen at the cineplex. Big enough to lead the Macy's Thanksgiving

Day Parade. The cord was his hair. The monstrous head was somehow pushing up the British ship and also becoming a part of it. A short section of mast protruded from his forehead. The tricolor British flag waved on his cheek like an animated tattoo.

Here was the really weird thing: The head seemed to be alive. The eyes moved, examining the scene and then seeming to concentrate on the *Constitution*. The eyes scanned the ship like King Kong looking for Fay Wray.

Jobs could feel the eyes looking directly at him. He could have sworn he saw a flicker of recognition. In his gut, Jobs knew this monstrous head belonged to Mo'Steel. The real thinking and feeling Mo'Steel. He didn't know whether to be happy or horrified.

Billy.

An awareness of Billy suddenly surged into Mo'Steel's consciousness.

Billy was there with him. Somehow Billy was holding him, somehow Billy was pulling him back.

Wait, Mo'Steel thought. *'Migo, a moment please!*

No use. He felt himself shrinking, falling. He hit ground in the basement, landing hard. He sat staring at the red beam, butt aching, and tried to get his breath. His stomach heaved, he had a nuclear head-ache, and every cell felt bruised.

Alive!

Mo'Steel laughed with pure joy and beat his chest like a gorilla in a bad movie. Like King Kong, in fact. He felt fantastic. He felt immortal. The Grim Reaper hadn't gotten him this time. He'd gone to dust and back and survived.

"Yahoooo!" he yelled. "I live."

Kubrick was watching him warily, keeping his distance. So the skinless wonder boy was scared of him. Now *that* was interesting. Alberto was still out of it and Billy didn't look much better. His face had that vacant, blind look he'd worn while comatose. Then — blink — the light and intelligence came back into his eyes.

"You okay?" Billy asked.

"Fantastic," Mo'Steel said. "Very substantial adrenaline rush." His mind was reeling, trying to make sense of what he'd seen. "Billy, you old freak, you saved my life!"

"I brought you back," Billy said.

"We were up there, right?" Mo'Steel said, pointing above his head to the environment.

Billy nodded.

"Well, I have to go back," Mo'Steel said immediately, urgently. "Only . . . can you pull me out like you did last time? Except this time I want you to wait until I give the sign."

"Yes," Billy said, although he sounded uncertain. "It isn't any more difficult than reading someone else's dream."

"Why do you want to go back?" Kubrick asked.

Mo'Steel almost said for the rush. No doubt, he was ready to try the ride again. But that wasn't the real, important reason.

"Our friends upstairs weren't doing too good," Mo'Steel explained. "Sounds weird, but it looks like some British warships are attacking them. They're getting hammered, taking on water. But up there, I'm big! And they could use a little Godzilla action to turn the battle around."

Nobody argued with him. Kubrick, Alberto, Billy — none of them seemed to care if he was in for a woolly ride.

That was just the way Mo'Steel liked it. Emotional arguments and hand-wringing just wasted a lot of time. He got up, brushed off his pants, and stepped back into the beam.

CHAPTER THIRTEEN

"THE KID'S GOT STYLE."

After Mo'Steel's enormous head disappeared, they fired the rest of the cannons. Jobs aimed at the Cartoons and took out maybe two dozen, maybe less. Seemed to slow them down a little.

"What now?" Edward asked.

Tate, too, was looking his way. And Roger Dodger. Even Anamull and D-Caf.

Jobs felt like a favorite baby-sitter who's run out of games. The truth was it didn't matter what they did. They were surrounded, out of ammo, and the ship was taking on water. Lots of water, judging from how far they were tilting to starboard. All that was left was to wait for the British to board them and try to fight them off.

Violet came down the ladder. "Are you guys busy?" she called. "Because we need help bailing! Find a bucket or anything that will hold water and head to the stern. Olga, T.R., and Burroway are already up there."

The littler kids hurried off to find buckets. Violet pulled Jobs aside. "Any ideas?" she asked in a low voice.

Jobs met Violet's gaze. She knew. Yeah, she definitely knew bailing was hopeless. Bailing was just an exercise she had dreamed up to keep people from panicking.

"The Cartoons will board sooner or later," Jobs said quietly. "We're outnumbered about forty to one. I don't think anything can save us, not even Tamara."

"Oh, well, in that case, I guess I'll do some bailing," Violet said with a wry smile.

"Yeah, bailing sounds like a good idea," Jobs said.

He hesitated. He felt as if he should say something to Violet. Something comforting. She looked scared. Waiting was hard. Waiting for the Cartoons to act and not knowing if they could protect themselves or if they were about to face death.

"Jobs!" Edward called, his voice squeaky with excitement. "Jobs, get up here now!"

Jobs and Violet ran for the ladder and scrambled up. They joined 2Face, Tate, Roger Dodger, and Edward. Yago and the others were standing nearby.

Mo'Steel.

He was back. His head had blossomed up from under another one of the British ships. Jobs watched in amazement as his shoulders and chest rose out of the water.

He was alive, or at least animated. He shook the water from his shoulder-length hair. Wrinkled his nose and sniffled with a sound like a freight train.

Once again, Jobs felt Mo'Steel's gaze fall on him. Not knowing know what else to do, Jobs waved.

"Romeo! Romeo, are you okay?" Olga was standing nearby, shouting up at her gargantuan son. He didn't seem to hear her. Olga fell to her knees, sobbing. Violet rushed forward to comfort her.

Everyone else stared upward silently. Awed.

Yago looked woozy. He had an angry red knot on his head. He must have fallen sometime during the battle.

Up and up, Mo'Steel rose. His waist appeared. His legs. He didn't stop growing until he was ankle-deep in the ocean water. He was impossibly big. As tall as a ten-story office tower. As tall as a Buddha carved into a mountainside.

Elements of the ship were superimposed on his flesh. His skin had the bumpy texture of sailcloth. A line of cannons ran diagonally across his chest like a bandolier, firing wildly, the cannonballs falling into the water.

Jobs struggled with the puzzle, but he couldn't crack it. His mind buzzed with questions. How could Mo'Steel still be alive? How was he appearing in this environment? And why? Did he need their help?

The giant Mo'Steel took a few steps, lifted his dump truck of a foot, and kicked in the side of one of the British ships. Water rushed into the gaping hole, the ship flipped onto its side, and it started to go down. Cartoon seamen threw themselves clear of the sinking ship.

"Yay, Mo'Steel!" Edward hollered.

Jobs was smiling, too. It looked as if the giant Mo'Steel was there to help them — not the other way around.

The *Constitution* rocked gently in the wake caused by Mo'Steel's steps. He was on the move again. Splashing over to another one of the British ships. This time he grasped the mainmast with one hand and pulled it loose. He threw the whole thing — mast, sails, rigging — into the ocean.

Now the entire group of ragged humans on the *Constitution* was cheering and shouting for Mo'Steel.

For the third ship, Mo'Steel bent his knees, lifted

one end of the ship out of the water, and flipped it over.

"Yahoo!" Edward yelled.

"Mo'Steel, Mo'Steel, he's our man!" Roger Dodger yelled.

Mo'Steel grinned and shook his hands overhead like a prizefighter. Then he took a deep bow and began to recede back into the ocean like a genie slipping back into a bottle.

"Admit it," Jobs said. "The kid's got style."

He wasn't talking to anyone in particular, but everyone nodded.

(CHAPTER FOURTEEN)

"MAYBE YOU'RE A SUPERHERO."

Mo'Steel landed on the floor with a back-jarring thud and sat there grinning like an idiot. "Oh, man, you should try this, Kubrick. It is beyond imagining, the woolliest ride in the universe."

"No thanks," Kubrick said coolly. Kubrick couldn't stand Mo's stupid grin. He acted as if this were all a game, a big joke.

Only a fool laughs in the face of death.

And, of course, Mo'Steel didn't even notice how the effort of bringing him back had exhausted Billy. Billy's face was expressionless, as always. But Kubrick could see that he was bathed in sweat and his skin was ashen.

"I decimated the Cartoons!" Mo'Steel said. "I stomped their boats like Tinkertoys. The few that survived are probably down on their hands and knees right now, praying to the Great Mo!"

"So your friends are safe now?" Kubrick asked.

Mo'Steel let out his breath and frowned. "The *Constitution* took some major damage. It looks like they're going down. And fast."

Kubrick stared up through the glass ceiling to the environment above. All sorts of debris were floating down through the water. Blasted pieces of wood. Scorched fabric. Even a battered cannonball that fell fast and bounced silently off the glass.

From below, Kubrick couldn't tell if the garbage was coming from the British ships or the *Constitution*. The bottom of one wood-hulled eighteenth-century ship looked pretty much like the next.

"So, let them sink," Kubrick said, suddenly feeling exhausted by all he'd had to endure. The people above were an abstraction to him. He'd met them briefly back on Earth before they'd boarded the shuttle. But they weren't his friends. And he wasn't really anxious to meet more strangers. More people who would stare and whisper behind his back.

"The ship will just vacuum them up like it vacuumed up the three of you," Kubrick went on harshly. "We can rescue your friends when they get down here."

"They'll never make it," Mo'Steel said, sounding very definite. "We only made it because Billy was with us. Actually, only two of us made it. Wylson blinked out somewhere on the way down."

"So what do you want to do?" Kubrick demanded, feeling his anger grow.

"You tell me," Mo'Steel said, shrugging.

Kubrick reached out and shoved Mo'Steel. Hard.

He hated being nagged for solutions, decisions. He'd spent his entire life being told he was incompetent and broken. Now he was suddenly supposed to be a leader?

Mo'Steel regained his balance quickly and stepped up to Kubrick. The two faced off, Mo'Steel watchful and Kubrick breathing heavily.

"We have to do this?" Mo'Steel asked.

Kubrick's dead-feeling hands twitched on his thighs.

Mo'Steel bent his knees slightly, rolled his head, met Kubrick's angry gaze. He wasn't afraid. Kubrick could see that in his expression. It heated his anger.

Wham! Kubrick brought up his fist and connected with Mo'Steel's jaw. A weight lifted.

Kubrick's father didn't react. He was down on his hands and knees, staring at his navel.

Kubrick caught flashes of fists. Mo'Steel hit his chest, his shoulder, his ribs. Kubrick felt the impact in his muscles.

The strange thing was that it didn't hurt. There was no pain, only a distant sort of sensation.

Getting hit was supposed to hurt.

Kubrick wanted it to hurt.

It didn't.

Kubrick dropped his fists, puzzlement beating out anger.

Mo'Steel watched warily. He moved in close, taking advantage of the opening, pummeling him. It was like being hit by a foam bat, like virtual-reality pain.

Mo'Steel finally dropped his fist. "Had enough?" he asked.

"I couldn't feel it," Kubrick said. He remembered his father's touch in the laboratory. He hadn't felt that, either. He'd begun to suspect this wasn't just some passing effect of his "operation." Now he knew.

Mo'Steel's eyes narrowed. "What do you mean?"

Billy, who had been hanging back, edged forward. He fixed his haunted eyes on Kubrick, listening.

Alberto pulled at his hair and mumbled, "Vega, Deneb, Sirius, Polaris, Pishpai, Dhur, 3 Lyrae, L^{2}Puppis, g Carinae, +38°3238, V4153 Sagitarii, GSC 1234 1132 . . ."

He's really losing it, Kubrick thought — and it made him angry all over again. His father had escaped. Abandoned him just like he always did. Now he'd have to pick up the pieces himself, cope alone.

"I can't feel pain through this — skin," Kubrick said.

Mo'Steel raised his eyebrows and slowly smiled. He looked at Kubrick with new respect. "Sounds like Mother gave you an upgrade," he said. There was no mistaking the envy in his voice.

"You think I should be happy?" Kubrick demanded. "Happy that machine turned me into a freak?"

"Maybe you're not a freak," Mo'Steel said. "Maybe you're a superhero. Impervious to pain. A living weapon. I wouldn't be surprised if Hollywood called to offer you a plasma screen show on Saturday morning. Oh, except for the fact that Hollywood is dust."

Mo'Steel envied him.

Kubrick could barely absorb that fact.

But what was even more disturbing was his own reaction: He was disappointed.

Disappointed he was strong.

Disappointed he was "impervious to pain."

Disappointed he would be hard to kill.

CHAPTER FIFTEEN

"TIME FOR THE LIFEBOATS."

The *Constitution* was going down fast.

Yago clung to the foremast with his left arm and tried to stay dry as waves crashed threateningly over the deck.

Black smoke billowed up from belowdecks. The ship's sails, shredded first by Blue Meanie fléchette guns and then by British cannonballs, flapped uselessly in the wind above him. The mainmast was down, the mizzen snapped in half. The weight of the massive beam pushed off-center was rolling the ship toward starboard. Air bubbled out of the gun ports as water rushed into the lower decks. The deck Yago stood on was rolled at a fun-house angle.

What a joke, Yago thought. For decades — no, for centuries — Revolution-crazed tourists had worshipped "Old Ironsides." Why? She was nothing but a death trap, in Yago's opinion. Wood that obviously sank like a stone, weighed down by heavy iron guns, yards of canvas sails, and a tangle of rigging.

Some of the others were bailing water out of the stern of the ship, the part that had sunk deepest into the water. Yago could see Violet working near the rail with Olga. T.R. and Edward were below-decks, passing ancient, leaking buckets up.

Their efforts were ridiculous, pitiful. The water they dumped out was only a hundredth, a thousandth, a millionth, of what poured in every second.

The ship was going down.

Yago needed a plan.

A plan to save himself.

Of course, he wanted the others to think he was concerned about each and every one of them. Too bad he had no clue how to save them.

And he had another worry: Tamara and the baby, the one remaining threat to his power.

Jobs came up the ladder from belowdecks and hurried toward Yago. "The bailing isn't helping," he said. "Time for the lifeboats."

"Of course it's time for the lifeboats," Yago said irritably, annoyed that Jobs seemed to think he hadn't thought of that. "Everyone to the lifeboats!"

he shouted out. "Jobs, figure out how to cut them loose."

Jobs ran forward. Violet, Olga, and the others abandoned their bailing. Everyone gathered in the cold, ankle-deep water and gazed down at the nearest boat. Tamara and the baby materialized from somewhere, giving Yago an uneasy feeling. He didn't like their secretive ways. He'd have to keep a closer eye on them.

"The boats are attached with a primitive sort of pulley system," Jobs said. "We should be able to untie this knot and lower the boats into the water."

"Great," Yago said. "Let's get aboard."

2Face held out a hand. "Not onto this one," she said, leaning precariously out over the water to examine the boat. "Fléchettes got it. Doesn't look seaworthy."

The group automatically began to move to the other side of the ship, slipping on the wet deck, sliding, hanging on to one another. This time, Yago made sure he — not that pushy 2Face — was the one to look brave checking out the boat.

"Okay, this one looks good," he announced. "Anamull, Jobs, stay on deck and lower us down once everyone is in." He chose carefully. Jobs because he would understand the rigging. Anamull for brute strength.

"Then how will they get into the lifeboat?" Violet argued.

"Down the rope," Yago said, although he really wasn't sure they could do it.

Jobs looked a little queasy, but he didn't argue. Anamull was too stupid to complain.

"One at a time," Yago commanded. "I'll go first."

Yago climbed over the rail and began lowering himself into the boat by holding on to the ropes securing it to the ship. The ropes were slippery. Yago lost his grip.

Fell.

Landed hard on the sloping deck on the boat and pitched forward onto his knees. A shooting pain shot through his right ankle and he got up slowly. The ankle throbbed. He'd twisted it. He limped to the closest bench and sat down.

Nobody seemed to notice his discomfort.

Olga was already coming down the rope.

Ten minutes later, they were all in. D-Caf had claimed the seat next to Yago. The benches weren't big enough for all of them so Tate, Roger Dodger, and Edward sat curled up on the deck.

Yago stared uneasily at Edward. His face, upper

arms, even his hair, had taken on a vague bluish cast like that of the brilliant sky behind him. A sharp line of demarcation ran across his chest. Any skin visible below that line was the mellow mahogany of old varnished wood. Chameleon boy.

Freak, D-Caf mouthed silently.

Yago nodded.

"Ready?" Jobs called from the ship deck.

"Do it!" Yago yelled. He was seriously irritable. His ankle hurt and the boat was much too crowded for his taste.

Jobs and Anamull fiddled with the ropes for a few seconds. Then, with a sudden, sickening lurch, the lifeboat dropped about two feet.

"Careful!" Yago yelled.

No response from above, but the lifeboat began to drop more smoothly. A few minutes later, they hit the water and Yago immediately noticed his feet were cold and wet.

Great.

"Water is coming in," Tate said. "Look, there's a hole in the boat." Her manner was almost casual as she pointed to a spot under Yago's bench.

"Start bailing!" Yago ordered.

"With what?" Tate asked.

"Didn't anyone bring a bucket?" Yago asked.

The others just stared back. The worst was the baby, who was looking at Yago with his hollow eyes and laughing. Obviously, the answer was no.

"Bail with your hands," Olga said nervously. "Someone stuff something into that hole!"

Yago sat still as the others scrambled to save the boat. He knew it was too late. He was already knee-deep in icy water. The only way to survive was to swim to the end of this environment. The border of the node might be a mile or ten miles away. The trick was to swim it before hypothermia set in.

They bailed with their hands. Jobs lowered pails down to them, and they switched to bailing with buckets.

Still, the boat sank lower and lower.

Olga was quivering with fear. She didn't say anything, but Yago saw her glassy stare, remembered how uneasy she'd been in the water before. This time would be even worse for her. This time she'd had time to panic.

The FBI had taught Yago what to do if any of the boats, helicopters, or planes he was riding in ever went down over water. Rule number one was to stay away from anyone who was panicking. A twitch could drown even the strongest swimmer.

Yago's gaze flickered to 2Face. He saw his opportunity. Took it.

"You're the strongest swimmer here," Yago said, ladling out the warm, caring tones that had been his mother's trademark. He spoke quietly, but loud enough so that Olga would overhear. "I want you to make sure Olga doesn't drown. You may be her only chance to survive this."

2Face stared back at him. Saw the trap. Said nothing.

One side of the boat slipped below the water. The boat filled quickly and sank straight down.

"Help!" Olga yelled.

Yago briefly went under.

Panic! Water pressing in from all around. No air. He was going to die. Suffocate! Suffocate under the freezing water. Then some minuscule part of his brain that was still rational, that hadn't been frozen by his claustrophobia, said: Kick.

Yago kicked and broke the surface, gasping for air.

Had anyone noticed? D-Caf. D-Caf was watching him.

"Start swimming," Yago snapped. "What are you waiting for?"

"I just wanted to make sure you were okay," D-Caf said.

"I'm fine," Yago said.

Turning his back on D-Caf, Yago took what his shrink called a "deep, cleansing breath." Then he reached down and slipped off his gym shoes. Tying the laces together, he wrapped them around his neck. Less chance of losing them that way.

Now he scanned the area for Tamara. There she was, baby clinging to her back, swimming purposefully toward the horizon.

That was the way to go.

CHAPTER SIXTEEN

"I AM ALSO INSANE."

"They are drowning," Billy said.

He concentrated, fighting to stay in the basement, where only three minds floated around him like angry bees. One worried but confident. One like a torrent of encrypted data streaming across a plasma screen. One tortured, simmering, explosive, implosive.

Three minds he could handle.

But if he let himself go, he would open himself to the swarm floating above. Fourteen minds screaming with fear. They were swimming or trying to swim, but the cold was numbing their fingers, freezing their toes, clouding their thoughts. They were tired and beginning to dream of resting, sinking.

Mo'Steel stared at him, frantic. "Maybe I can help them," he said. "Maybe I — I could . . . when the beams come back again. I could go huge and pick them out of the water."

"Then what?" Kubrick demanded. "How are you going to get them back here?"

"I don't know!" Mo'Steel exploded.

"You can't help," Billy said. "They will be gone by the time the beams come back on."

"How does he know this stuff?" Kubrick muttered.

"He knows," Mo'Steel said. "That's the thing. Don't worry about how. Billy, 'migo, I think you're our only hope. Can you do something?"

"Like what?" Kubrick said. "It's hopeless."

"Like dry up the ocean!" Mo'Steel shouted. "Like give the people up there wings! I don't know — something! Because I'm telling you, no offense, but I don't much like the idea of being stuck with the three of you for the rest of eternity. For instance, some fems would be nice. One at the very least. Billy, I'm begging you, do something."

Only one possibility. Billy glanced at Alberto, touched his mind. Billy had learned on the long voyage how to access someone else's mindscape. He tried firing the neurons nestled among the gray matter in Alberto's skull. Only 87.6 percent of the billions of switches in Alberto's mind responded.

The rest were fried.

Obliterated.

Somehow Billy sensed they'd been killed not by the power of Mother's mind, not by her vastness, but by her madness. As Billy watched, he could see more switches sizzle and go dark. It was like watching a computer virus wipe out an operating system.

"Maybe I can dry up the ocean," Billy said.

"How?" Mo'Steel demanded.

"Connect with Mother and redirect her programming."

Now Mo'Steel glanced at Alberto. His eyes were darting wildly back and forth, back and forth. A strand of drool glistened on his lower lip. "Won't you — end up like that?"

"I don't know," Billy said.

He knew he had to try. The swarm of minds above were losing out to the cold. They were beginning to feel sleepy, to relax, to drift off. The people who had carried him for many miles, protected him, rescued him.

Mo'Steel's mother was up there. Billy could feel Mo'Steel's fear for her.

He had to try.

"We'd better use the same pit as before," Mo'Steel said. The bee that was his mind rose as if on a draft of warm air. He was hopeful. "We know that one is active."

Mo'Steel began to jog. So did Billy.

Kubrick grabbed Billy's hand, squeezing him painfully, and pulled him to a stop. "Don't be stupid!" he said. "One jabbering fool around here is enough. We don't need to make the same mistake twice."

Billy stared into Kubrick's intense eyes, almost wishing Kubrick would convince him not to try. He was afraid. Afraid to feel again, afresh, all the horrors of long isolation.

He'd been alone for five hundred years.

The question was: How long had Mother been alone?

Millennia, maybe.

"It is not the same as with your father," Billy said. "I think Mother and I have something in common."

"What could you have in common with that awful machine?" Kubrick demanded. "She's corrupt — insane!"

"I am also insane," Billy said.

Kubrick snatched his hand back, narrowing his eyes. Billy sensed Kubrick's mind turn against him at the same time his expression shut down. Billy could feel and see his disgust.

"Let's go!" Mo'Steel barked from a few paces away.

Billy turned and followed Mo'Steel.

Kubrick lagged behind, pushing Alberto ahead of him, no longer afraid of the beams.

They jogged. The only sounds were the slap of their feet on the smooth floor and Alberto's vague, endless rambling.

Billy felt as if they were moving dangerously, impossibly fast. He was aware of his joints bending, his pores sweating. He kept his mind closed to the cacophony of horrified thoughts swirling above him. Tried not to keep counting the consciousnesses, making sure they were all there.

They arrived at the pit. Mo'Steel helped Billy into the exact chair that had turned Alberto into a lunatic. Billy sat on the edge, legs dangling. For a moment, his eyes locked onto Mo'Steel's worried, hopeful gaze.

He sat back.

Music filled his ears.

CHAPTER SEVENTEEN

"YOU WANT FRIES WITH THAT?"

Someone suddenly changed the channel.

The churning, frigid ocean disappeared. Jobs found himself standing in a bleak city square. In front of him was a building of gray concrete, maybe ten stories tall. All of the windows were blown out.

Salt water from his clothes dripped onto rubble. Small shards of jagged concrete. Ripped and stained pieces of Sheetrock. Rusty nails. A pink sofa, over-turned, curved legs sticking up. A smashed-open refrigerator with chicken bones, lettuce, and beets spilling out and rotting in the sun.

Jobs coughed and gagged. He covered his mouth and nose with his hand to block the smell.

Here and there, people wandered alone or in groups of two or three. They kept their eyes down as if they were looking for something — or some-one — in the rubble.

Nearby, an elderly woman dressed in a black winter coat and a black shawl. She was sobbing and dabbing at her eyes with a handkerchief. Jobs knew from the way her mouth was caved in that she didn't have any teeth, not even false ones.

Off to the right, a pale boy with angry eyes, an angry mouth, staring hostilely and unwaveringly at Jobs. "вы можете мне помочь найти мою маму?" the boy asked.

Jobs didn't understand. He looked away.

This "environment" was different from the other ones Mother had created, Jobs told himself. Thinking, analyzing the situation calmed him. For one thing, this environment didn't feel painterly or imaginative. It had the gritty detail of a newsreel, or reality. The people weren't Cartoons. They were definitely three-dimensional.

For another thing, it was cold. A bitter wind blew across the ruined square, tossing up pieces of soggy newsprint. Jobs shivered in his wet clothes. His fingers, toes, and nose were numb from the cold seawater and the wind wasn't doing much to warm him up.

Off in the distance, beyond the bombed-out building, Jobs could see a towering dome. He squinted and thought he could make out a tiny

Statue of Liberty on top. The dome was bathed in warm sunlight and Jobs could clearly see an American flag fluttering at its base.

Where were the other Remnants? Was he stuck in this nightmare alone? Where was Edward? His little brother was his responsibility now. He had to find him, protect him.

Jobs shoved his hands in his pockets and started across the square toward the dome. Maybe the others, wherever they were, would see the American flag and head in that direction.

Then the sound track kicked in.

Overhead! A powerful motor, a howling wind, and a *fa-whop, fa-whop, fa-whopping*. Instinctively, Jobs fell to his knees and covered his head with his arms. He cowered, the rubble biting into his knees, and looked up.

An attack helicopter. Black and deadly looking. Russian — guessing from the Cyrillic lettering on the side.

Machine-gun fire! Hitting a piece of Sheetrock not two feet away, making it dance. Jobs hid his face. Ridiculous, pointless — he should be running for cover! — but he was too frightened, too disoriented.

The machine-gun fire was replaced by a high-pitched wailing that made Jobs suck in his breath.

Then — an explosion so loud it seemed to have weight, substance. The ground shook. Jobs was thrown sideways, the breath knocked out of him. He clawed at his burning ears, trying to block out the sound. Tried, at the same time, to fill his lungs with air.

Then — another wail, another explosion.

And another.

And another.

Jobs curled into a ball, sobbing, praying for it to end.

The ocean disappeared and 2Face found herself in a damp, chilly basement. The rest of the Remnants were gone.

2Face was huddling with a strange, dark-haired little girl in what appeared to be a coal bin. They were squashed together. 2Face could smell the girl's hair. She could feel the little girl's wool coat scratching against her still-damp arm.

Weird, 2Face thought as she studied the girl in the dim light coming through one grimy window.

She seemed so real. Not like the Cartoons on the British ships. So many details. A tiny mole on the border of her upper lip. Pierced ears with gold-and-

117

red Minnie Mouse earrings. Pulse beating rapidly in her neck. For a moment, 2Face wondered if she was one of the Remnants who had disappeared from the shuttle. But no. They hadn't had anyone this young among them.

Outside, 2Face could hear heavy machinery moving down the street. Tanks? 2Face couldn't be sure.

"What's that —" she started to ask.

The little girl reached over and covered 2Face's mouth with a small, filthy hand. Her eyes were wild as she shook her head forcefully.

2Face got the message: They were supposed to be quiet.

Fine.

She closed her eyes and took a couple of deep breaths. After fighting Olga in the waves, she was tired. Tired and hungry. Famished, actually. The last thing she'd eaten was a moldy, dry hunk of bread on the *Constitution*. And that was — what? Six hours ago? Eight?

What happened to Olga anyway? 2Face hoped she wasn't still in the water. She'd drown without someone to help her.

A door opened with a creak. It was one of those cellar doors that led directly outside. A bulkhead.

Feet came down the three steps into the basement. Black lace-up boots. Black pants. Two men talking in a guttural language.

The little girl pulled 2Face deeper into the shadows. All 2Face could see were the whites of her wide-open eyes. The men were wearing fur collars and hats. They stomped around, turning over boxes and poking into corners with their rifles.

2Face held her breath, but one of the men had already spotted them. He laughed and nudged his companion.

The little girl squashed herself against the rough stone wall. One of the soldiers grabbed her roughly by the arm. She screamed as he pulled her from her hiding place.

"Stop!" 2Face reached out for the little girl. But she was growing fuzzy, indistinct.

Alarmed, 2Face looked at the soldier. His scratchy whiskers disappeared, replaced by a terrible case of acne. Good-bye, fur hat, black uniform, and assault rifle. Now he was wearing a red-and-white-striped shirt, a blue baseball cap with a yellow M stitched on it, and a yellow plastic name tag that read IVAN.

"You want fries with that?" Ivan asked.

2Face blinked. She saw fluorescent lighting, a linoleum counter, soda machines. The place was instantly recognizable. McDonald's. Exactly like the one in Miami Beach where she and her friends hung out when they were skipping school. The familiar smell was enough to almost make her faint with joy.

"Yeah," 2Face said. "Supersize them. And give me a large Coke, a carton of milk, a hot apple pie — and, um, a side salad." She'd never ordered salad in McDonald's before, but how bad could it be? She was starving.

Ivan punched the keys and then began to fill her order.

2Face turned to have a look around.

She screamed.

Behind her was a soldier. Not a Russian. He was thinner and less well equipped than the pair from the basement. His dark beard was full. He had a bloody rag wrapped around his head. He leaned on his rifle, shifting his weight impatiently as he waited his turn to order.

Behind the soldier was a teenage kid wearing very expensive Nikes and reading a battered copy of *My Àntonia*. A drop of the soldier's blood splattered the kid's shoes.

Behind the kid, the line stretched on. The lunch rush. A weird mix of suburban kids and bloody soldiers sporting a variety of raw flesh wounds, wearing tall hats and heavy capes.

2Face was shaking.

"Here you go," Ivan said, pushing a tray her way. "Enjoy your meal. Thank you for visiting McDonald's."

"Thanks," 2Face said, relieved she didn't have to pay. She forced herself to concentrate on that. Right, think about the free meal. Ignore the men, especially the one whose nose had been blasted away, exposing a gaping dark hole.

2Face picked up her tray and steered around the line, keeping her eyes on her fries, wishing she had thought to ask for ketchup.

"Yo — 2Face!"

Jobs, Yago, Edward, and Violet were sitting together at a booth, looking exhausted and half wet. The table was littered with balled-up burger wrappers and empty fry containers.

2Face slid into a seat. "Where are we?" she asked.

"In the middle of someone's nightmare," Jobs said.

"Yeah — but whose?" 2Face spotted a ketchup packet on someone's tray and grabbed it. She was determined to eat before she was dumped into some new horror show.

Violet gazed thoughtfully out the restaurant's window. The view was of a parking lot. Sport utilities and minivans parked in neat rows with an occasional armored tank rolling past. Beyond the parking lot, 2Face could see a low-slung, flat-roofed building that had to be a school. Maybe the high school all the kids in line attended.

"We should get together as much food as we can easily carry," Yago said. "Edward, get in line and place a to-go order. Try to get something that will taste good cold. No fish sandwiches."

"Sure, boss around the little kid," Edward said sullenly. But he got up and joined the line. He studiously gazed away from the soldier in front of him, who held a severed leg in both hands.

"Have you seen Tamara and the baby?" Yago asked 2Face.

"No," 2Face said, reluctant to talk to Yago, but seeing no way to avoid it. "She's probably off engaging in a little recreational hand-to-hand combat. Or shopping at Eyeless Babies R Us."

"Hey, kid!" Yago called to Edward. "Get me a chocolate shake." He pushed the garbage to one side of the table and put his feet up. "Oh, man, this is a dream come true. All I need now is a little HBO."

"Do you mind?" 2Face asked. "I'm trying to eat."

Yago closed his eyes and sighed contentedly. "No, Freak, I don't mind. Go ahead and eat."

Ignore him, 2Face told herself. *Ignore him until you can make him eat dirt.*

"Do you recognize this artist?" 2Face asked Violet, between enormous bites of her Big Mac. Nothing — not even Yago — could make her lose her appetite.

"No," Violet said. "Contemporary art has never been a particular interest of mine. I'd guess someone created this tableau in the last years before Earth's destruction. The juxtaposition of a war zone and mundane American life is really quite affecting."

Jobs raised his eyebrows. "Yeah, affecting," he mumbled. "Um, I also noticed that all the cars have Texas license plates. Well, not the tanks."

"So?" 2Face asked.

"So maybe whoever is creating this environment is from Texas," Jobs said. "Texas and a war zone."

"Isn't Billy from Texas?" Violet asked. "I remember his father wearing cowboy boots."

Jobs nodded. "And he's an orphan from somewhere in Eastern Europe."

123

"What do you mean whoever is creating this environment?" Yago asked impatiently. "I thought the ship's computer was doing it, using data chips or whatever."

"The other environments, yes," Jobs said. "But this one is different. It feels more real."

"Yes!" Violet said. "This environment is much more vivid than the others. The people don't seem like Cartoons. They're three-dimensional. They breathe."

"Edward!" Yago yelled. "Make that shake vanilla."

"Jobs!" Edward yelled.

"Just do it, kid," Yago yelled. "Why does everything have to be a big debate with you?"

"Jobs, you'd better get over here now!" Edward yelled.

CHAPTER EIGHTEEN

"ARE YOU SURE THIS IS THE KINGDOM YOU WANT TO COMMAND?"

Jobs was on his feet. So were 2Face and Violet. They rushed toward the counter, jostling soldiers and schoolkids, leaving Yago scrambling to catch up.

The wage slaves behind the counter had disappeared. And, as Jobs looked on, they were being replaced.

Behind the registers appeared a monster with see-through skin. He looked warily around, a gory Saturday-morning-TV bad guy brought to life.

"Ya-ahh!" Jobs cried.

"Whoa!" Yago yelled.

"Careful!" Jobs held his arms out to stop Edward from getting too close.

The monster stared contemptuously at Jobs with a reptile's green eyes. "Don't worry, I don't bite."

Jobs's insides went liquid as he realized this monster might be human. He didn't seem like a Cartoon, like part of the environment. Lord, could this be one of the Remnants?

"Great," Yago said. "Just what we need. More freaks."

A man appeared next to the deep fryer. Jobs recognized him as one of the Wakers they'd abandoned on the shuttle. Only the guy looked as if he'd aged ten years since then. His head was twitching back and forth, eyes unfocused.

Mo'Steel appeared next. He was sitting on the counter, arms crossed over his chest, swinging his feet, grinning.

"Yo, Jobs!" Mo said. "Glad to see you didn't turn into a big Popsicle, 'migo. So. This is pretty twisted, huh?"

Jobs was so relieved to see his friend that he had to fight an urge to hug him. But he also felt uneasy. Was Mo'Steel real?

Mo didn't look quite right. Jobs had seen the steel-gray T-shirt he was wearing a hundred times on Earth and since they woke up. The left sleeve had a hole in it where Mo'Steel hit a sharp rock while mountain climbing in Yosemite. Only now the hole was gone.

"Where did you come from?" Jobs asked warily. "What's going on?"

"I hate to wig you out, Duck," Mo'Steel said. "But I think we're inside Billy Weir's head."

"Then Billy could definitely use some time on the couch," 2Face said. She was looking at the monster boldly, trying to hide her disgust. "He's got some sick stuff going on in his mind."

Mo'Steel laughed. "Don't blame Billy — that's reality. Everyone, meet Kubrick."

Jobs looked back at the monster and studied him closely. He'd met Kubrick briefly on the shuttle, before the worms had come. He'd looked normal then. So who had turned him into this monster? And why?

"What happened to you?" Violet whispered.

Kubrick only glared at her. He practically glowed with hostility. He made Jobs uneasy on more than one level. Scary and sporting a bad attitude. Trouble.

"I thought Billy drowned," Jobs said, still having a hard time believing his friend was alive.

Mo'Steel nodded. "It looked bad for a few seconds there. Then Billy surrounded me and Wylson in some sort of air bubble until we were safe and sound. I think the ship thought we were garbage."

"Are you telling me Wylson's alive?" Yago demanded.

Mo'Steel's gaze moved to Violet. "Um, no. I guess — by the time Billy got to her it was too late. I'm sorry, Violet."

Jobs glanced at Miss Blake. She met his gaze evenly, eyes dry. Jobs felt like he should say something. But what? He'd noticed Violet and her mother avoided each other. They seemed locked in some private battle.

Then there was the fact that so many had already died. Both of Jobs's own parents. The six or seven billion people they'd abandoned on Earth. If they stopped now to mourn for Wylson, how would they ever stop?

Violet cleared her throat. "You said we were inside Billy's head? How is that possible?"

"He's interfacing with Mother," Mo'Steel said. "Programming her. It was the only way we could save you guys from drowning."

"You found the bridge?" Jobs demanded eagerly.

"No," Mo'Steel said uncertainly. "Just a sort of computer interface."

"Good enough," Jobs said urgently. "Maybe it can help us get control of this situation. Mo, lead the way. Come on, everyone!"

"Hang on a second," Yago said. "I'm in charge here. And nobody is going anywhere until I say so."

"Give it a rest, Yago," 2Face said impatiently. "We're in a fast-food restaurant conjured up by a very sick mind. Are you sure this is the kingdom you want to command?"

Suddenly, as if on some unspoken command, all of the soldiers in the restaurant dropped into defensive postures. They crawled under tables on their bellies. They loaded and cocked their rifles and aimed them at the main entrance.

The schoolkids who had been mixed in among the soldiers faded and disappeared. All except one. A big kid — a kid who looked like he could do some damage with his fists and enjoy it.

"What's happening?" 2Face asked.

"I don't know, but it doesn't look good," Jobs said.

"Take cover," Yago commanded. "Everyone behind the counter. Pronto."

Nobody argued. They raced behind the counter and crouched down. Kubrick roughly pulled his father to his knees. Jobs got Edward in front of him and then peeked up to see what was happening.

A force was invading.

First came a half-dozen pale men and women dressed in heavy silk-and-brocade clothing. The women's dresses brushed the floor. One of the men wore what looked to Jobs like a black sombrero ringed with red and yellow flowers. The women's heads were covered with lacy scarves or brilliant feathered hats.

Jobs relaxed a hair. "They don't look dangerous," he said.

"They aren't even armed," Edward said.

"Get down," Jobs said, giving his little brother's head a push.

"The gorgeous color in their clothes . . . they look like Vermeers," Violet said in wonder. "But that doesn't make sense. Why would the soldiers be afraid of a few Dutch noblemen?"

Apparently the soldiers weren't taking any chances.

They opened fire.

"Score one for the insurgent rebel dudes," Yago said.

But now a very different force sprang up at the entrance. They were creatures ripped from the covers of cheap science fiction p-books.

A thin, heavily muscled woman with flowing blond hair stepped forward. She wore only a teeny bikini that seemed to be made of beads and wire. No shoes. Her skin glistened with oil.

She carried an ornate weapon. One side was pointed like a lance. A glittering blade shaped like an oversized ax topped the other side.

Jobs wasn't the type to whistle at pretty girls. But he shot a glance at Mo'Steel, who winked back.

"These chicks are from Billy's memory?" 2Face asked.

"They look like Cartoons," Violet said. "Look. The soldiers are more realistic, detailed. The warriors are sketchy, two-dimensional like the Brueghel figures or the demons were."

"That's because Billy only imagined them," Yago said.

"No," Jobs said. "At least, I don't think so. I think the computer is resisting Billy. I think she's using these, um, these —"

"Hot warrior chicks," Kubrick supplied.

"Yes," Jobs said. "Using these warriors and Vermeers to fight Billy's soldiers."

The warrior woman smiled. "You find me attractive," she said. "Perhaps that leads you to underestimate my strength." She sprang forward.

Laughing, the warrior pointed her weapon at the kids huddled behind the counter.

"Get them!" she yelled.

(CHAPTER NINETEEN)

"TROUBLE."

The warrior advanced, swinging her ax.

Violet watched in awe, simultaneously sickened and impressed by the warrior's brute strength.

Behind the first warrior came a dozen more, all women. They were longhaired and dressed in tight, scanty clothing. Their weapons were brutish and medieval, but they were getting the job done.

The soldiers regained their senses and started to fire. Violet saw a black-haired warrior wearing thigh-high leather boots take a bullet in her stomach. She seemed to evaporate into thin air.

Other warriors disappeared, too.

But new ones kept rushing through the door, barefoot. Violet didn't know who had painted these warriors, but she wouldn't have called him — it had to be a him — an "artist." They leaped up on the red-and-white tables, thrusting their spears and axes, shouting joyously when one of the soldiers fell. By sheer force of numbers, they were winning the battle.

"We need a back door!" 2Face said urgently.

Violet, who had been mesmerized by the battle raging around her, snapped back to reality. She followed 2Face and Mo'Steel, back toward the frying machines and grills. They raced past the huge stainless refrigerators and came to a sudden halt.

Behind the machines, the detail of their surroundings tapered off. The back of the restaurant was nothing but a blank white cinder-block wall.

No back entrance.

Kubrick let out a shout of frustration and punched the solid wall with his fist. He didn't even flinch.

"This environment is based on Billy's memories," Jobs reminded them. "I guess he never got back this far."

"Now what?" 2Face asked Yago. "You wanted to be in charge. Now would be a real good time for you to make a useful suggestion."

"I'm thinking!" Yago snapped.

"They're getting closer," Edward said, fearfully looking back toward the dining room.

Violet had an idea.

An idea born of all the nights her parents had taken her to McDonald's, or a place like it, to eat dinner at nine P.M. This was supposed to be their "family time" — the twenty minutes her mother spent with Violet and her father after working a fourteen-hour day and before rushing home to answer her link messages and e-mail.

Violet's mother had spent her whole life working. She'd spent her whole life making money and impressing people with her work ethic.

She'd probably imagined the *New York Times* would print an obituary when she died. Maybe there'd be a quick mention in *Business World* magazine: "Billionaire Software Titan Mourned."

And yet . . . and yet it seemed odd not to have her mother marching around barking orders. To know that she would never do that again.

"We could escape through the drive-through window," Violet said. Her voice was mostly drowned out by the grunts and moans of battle coming from the dining area.

2Face heard. She stared at Violet for a moment, then smiled and yelled, "Drive-through!"

They ran.

Violet was relieved to see the drive-through fully imagined. One by one, they pulled themselves up through the small sliding window and dropped down onto the driveway beneath.

Alberto posed a bit of a problem. Violet didn't know what had happened to him — nobody had taken the time to explain — but it was easy enough to see he was crazy. Kubrick yelled at him, begged him, ordered him to climb up. But he kept wandering off, jabbering. He didn't seem to hear, or maybe he couldn't understand.

Violet felt sorry for Alberto. She'd often wondered — since they'd woken up to find so many of their loved ones dead and their own lives in constant jeopardy — how many of them were close to losing their minds.

She didn't step forward to help as Mo'Steel and Kubrick grabbed Alberto and pushed him through the window headfirst. Jobs and 2Face grabbed Alberto's shoulders and pulled him through from the other side.

Mo'Steel and Kubrick quickly followed. Their little group huddled together on the pavement, looking fearfully around them. The battle raged on inside the restaurant. The warriors weren't following them. At least, not yet.

Violet gazed across the parking lot at the high school. A few minutes ago when they were eating, it had been whole, peaceful. Now it was nothing but a bombed-out shell, windows shattered, smoke rising.

Even the sky was in turmoil. One second it was bright blue and sunny. The next second, threatening dark clouds churned, thunder lashed, and bitter-cold rain pelted them. Then, just as suddenly, the blue sky came back.

"Watch out!" 2Face yelled.

Violet looked down and saw the pavement had begun to bubble. The mixture of tar and rocks was heating up. Violet's shoes sank into the gooey mess.

"The grass!" Jobs yelled. "Get on the grass."

Edward was the first to hop onto a sun-scorched patch of grass rimming the parking lot. The others followed quickly, Kubrick pulling his father to safety.

But now Violet saw the grass undulate. Something was burrowing through it, pushing up dirt.

She thought instantly of the worms. The worms had attacked them when they first got off the shuttle and killed Big Bill. The sensation of a worm tunneling into her right index finger came vividly back to her.

No, she could not let the worms get her again.

Trembling, terrified, Violet scrambled up onto the hood of a nearby car. Fear sent her up over the windshield and onto the roof. Only when she was safe could she think about the others. "Worms. Worms — or something!" she called. "Get off the grass."

But the others had already noticed. Jobs and Mo'Steel climbed onto a red SUV next to her. The rest managed to get up onto the flatbed of a nearby pickup truck.

Edward climbed onto the roof of the truck's cab and stood up. Violet shook her head. They were facing death and Edward was playing King of the Hill. But then she saw Edward was scanning the horizon.

"Look!" he yelled. "I think I see the others!"

There they were! Across the street, only a few hundred yards away. Tamara, the baby, and Anamull were out front. Then came D-Caf, Tate, and Roger Dodger. Mo'Steel's mom, Burroway, and T.R. were last. They were running up the stone path of a large, stately church that had appeared in place of one of the bombed-out buildings. The women warriors were after them. One of the armored tanks was providing cover. But three warriors, mounted on what looked like small dragons, were closing in on the tank and surrounding it.

"It's all right," Jobs said. "They're going to make it."

Then Violet noticed something that made her catch her breath.

Riders.

They were coming down the street, paying no attention to the stop signs. At least a dozen of the rust-colored, two-headed aliens zooming toward them on their hoverboards.

Violet felt an urgent need to run and hide. But run where? She didn't want to touch the grass that surrounded the parking lot. Where could they go?

Next to her, Violet heard Jobs moan deeply.

"What's up, Duck?" Mo'Steel called.

Jobs was pointing to the sky — to what Violet first thought was a flock of geese flying high overhead.

"What?" Kubrick called. "What is that?"

"Squids," Jobs said.

"Trouble," Mo'Steel said.

CHAPTER TWENTY

"<u>CHEZ</u> WEIRD, I PRESUME."

"We need cover!" Jobs yelled.

"The church!" Yago yelled.

2Face spun around in a full circle. But now the church was gone, replaced by a carousel. For a moment, 2Face stood, stunned, and watched the brightly painted horses moving smoothly up and down. A child's terrified wail competed with the cheerful organ music. 2Face put her hands over her ears and tried to think. How could they pick a place to hide when the landscape was constantly shifting? It was like trying to make sense of a bad dream.

Edward screamed.

"Ah-hhh!" 2Face yelled.

The flatbed of the truck was filled with cockroaches. Hundreds of them, thousands, millions. So many that they poured over the edges of the flatbed. Small ones. Big ones. Tan, brown, black. They were crawling over one another, moving up onto the cab, toward 2Face and the others.

2Face heard their hard bodies rustling as they scurried along. Her nose filled with their spicy, acrid smell.

The car Violet was standing on was packed full of them. Filled so that the windows were dark, no crack of light visible.

"Time to go!" 2Face called.

"Look!" Mo'Steel yelled.

A house had appeared on the other side of the carousel. A mansion of tan stone with elaborate windows and tasteful landscaping. A soft golden sunlight warmed its red-tiled roof.

2Face scrambled down off the truck, forcing herself to ignore the bugs under her fingers, the bugs crawling across her arms, heading for her ears, her nose, her mouth. She hit the ground and ran, vaguely aware the others were following her. All she could think about was getting to the house before it vanished.

Mo'Steel got to the front door first. He paused for a moment before trying the door.

2Face laughed with relief when the doorknob turned and the door swung open, revealing an expanse of marble tiling and a grand staircase leading to the second floor.

They crowded into the entranceway. Jobs, the last inside, closed and locked the door. 2Face tried to catch her breath, shake off the creepies. She wasn't helped by the fact that Kubrick was watching her with his penetrating eyes. Why was he always staring at her?

"*Chez* Weird, I presume," Yago said.

"What makes you think that?" 2Face asked.

"Billy is in control — or at least partly in control — of this environment," Jobs said. "It makes sense that he'd think of his own home as a safe place to be."

"And besides, this place is just so Texas *nouveau riche*," Yago said. "Big and tasteless."

Yago had a point. The place was too big. Miles of plush carpet and expensive tiles. The furniture looked lost in the oversized rooms. All except the plasma screen, which was big enough for the local multiplex.

Kubrick gave his father a little push so that he sat down on a smooth leather couch. Then he began to prowl around the room, looking for who knows what.

Violet went into the living room and peered through the double-height windows. "No sign of the Riders or the warriors. Or the bugs," she added with a little shudder.

"Keep a lookout," Yago told her. "Mo, go into the kitchen. Check out the backyard."

2Face was sickened to see Violet and Mo'Steel do what Yago ordered. She couldn't let the others accept Yago as their leader. Impossible! She'd never survive under his leadership. But what could she do? For now, nothing. Except maybe resist his leadership herself.

"Come on, Edward," 2Face said. "Yago doesn't have any orders for us freaks. Let's go see what's in the fridge."

2Face followed Edward into the kitchen, where they found Mo'Steel and Jobs staring warily into the backyard. More graceful landscaping — this time surrounding a pool big enough to train the U.S. Olympic swim team.

"What happened to Alberto?" Jobs was asking as they came in.

"Bad trip," Mo'Steel explained. "He connected with Mother and she blew his mind."

"But Billy," Jobs said. "Isn't he in danger?"

"Billy is in a squeaky spot," Mo'Steel admitted.

Edward opened the fridge. "Ew!"

"What's wrong?" 2Face asked.

Edward pointed inside the fridge. "Look."

The fridge was full of row after row of cracked bowls filled with what looked like greenish oatmeal. "Weird," 2Face said. "But why not? This place is totally wacko."

Jobs looked over 2Face's shoulder. "We'd better be careful," he said thoughtfully. "This house might be booby-trapped."

"Say what?" Edward asked.

"In case you haven't figured it out already, Mother and Billy are fighting for control of this node," Jobs explained. "Let's assume Billy created this house as a safe place for us to hide. We can guess he wouldn't put slimy oatmeal in the fridge. It follows that Mother has control over parts of this environment."

"Why oatmeal?" 2Face asked. "Why not brussels sprouts or plastic explosives?"

Job shrugged. "Like you said, this place is wacko."

"Duh," Edward said. "You think you're so smart, Sebastian. But you miss things that are so obvious."

"What?" 2Face demanded.

143

"Mother is reading Billy's mind," Edward said. "She found out he hates oatmeal so that's what she puts in the fridge. She's . . . she's acting out."

2Face and Jobs laughed.

Edward's face turned red. "That's what Mom calls it — called it — when I did stuff like that!"

"Squids!" Mo'Steel yelled.

The three of them spun toward the window. "Where?"

"Taking a dip," Mo'Steel said.

2Face got to the window in time to see the last of them slide under the water, tentacle arms waving. She would have sworn they were bigger and more vividly colored than the Squids they'd fought from the *Constitution*. "What are they up to?" she asked.

Mo'Steel shrugged. Edward looked concerned. Even Jobs could only shake his head.

2Face didn't have much time to ponder this puzzle. The floor under Edward suddenly erupted like Old Faithful. Edward fell back against the counter, clutching his right leg, eyes full of tears.

"What is it? What happened?" Jobs demanded.

"I don't know," Edward said.

The eruptions continued. They came in a line like a row of stitches down the floor. The tile floor turned to liquid and burst upward. A new line erupted above the sink. Each blast sent shards of ceramic tile flying.

As usual, Jobs got it first. "The Squids!" he yelled. "They must be in the plumbing. Remember how they distorted matter at the statue? They're doing it again. Stay away from pipes, water faucets, anything to do with the plumbing."

They ran back into the living room to warn the others. "Squids in the plumbing!" Edward announced.

Yago was standing in the middle of the living room, looking lost and uncertain. "A gun. Wouldn't you think Big Bill would have a gun somewhere?"

"The Riders," Violet explained. "They're at the front door."

Things got quiet as everyone watched the front doorknob jangle. *Maybe the lock would stop the Riders,* 2Face thought desperately. *Maybe they'd never seen a doorknob before.*

The doorbell rang.

"Don't answer that," Yago ordered.

CHAPTER TWENTY-ONE

"THE SAFEST PLACE SHOULD BE
UNDER THE COVERS."

"They're coming around!" Violet announced. "Examining the windows. I think they're coming through!"

2Face remembered the Rider attack when they were in the tower. "Get upstairs!" she yelled. "They have a problem with stairs."

Everyone ran. A panicked flight. Yago. Then 2Face and Violet. Jobs helping Edward. Kubrick dragging his father. Mo'Steel bringing up the rear.

Yago took a quick right into one of the bedrooms and they all followed. Billy's room. Had to be. Dallas Cowboys wallpaper. A shelf of expensive-looking stuffed animals, all with a brand-new, never-been-hugged perfection. Navy carpeting. A stack of data disks on the desk next to a computer that had been brand-new in 2011.

"Weapons!" Yago yelled. "See if you can find anything sharp or pointy or dangerous."

From downstairs, the sound of shattering glass. The Riders were inside.

"I wish Tamara were here," Yago muttered. "Tamara knows how to deal with these guys."

2Face yanked one of the louvered closet doors. She reached for a baseball bat that was lying on the floor among a bunch of dirty laundry. Her fingers closed on it and then —

"Ah-hhh!" 2Face screamed.

A monster had jumped out of the closet's shadows. A big plush, purple carpet-covered monster with googly red eyes. He looked like one of the Wild Things. He reached out his short arms and grabbed 2Face's neck with his six-fingered hands. His breath smelled like rotten eggs.

2Face wiggled free. She slammed the door closed and leaned against it. A clown on the shelf pointed at 2Face and laughed maniacally.

Things were getting seriously twisted.

The teddy bears had come alive and advanced to the edge of the shelf. They snarled and pawed the ground, searching for a way down the smooth wall.

Inhuman eyes glowed from under the bed. Every so often, a sickly green-skinned hand would reach out from that dark space and snatch wildly into the air.

The Squids were attacking through the floor and the walls adjoining the bathroom. One of the blasts had gotten Alberto. He was bleeding from his head.

And the Riders were coming. The stairs wouldn't slow them for long.

"Edward, get on the bed," 2Face ordered. "Get everyone who doesn't have a weapon on the bed. Mother is creating these monsters from Billy's childhood fears. The safest place should be under the covers."

Yago sneered. "Good plan. Why doesn't someone turn on the night-light while you're at it."

Edward obeyed immediately. Mo'Steel and Jobs picked up Alberto by the arms and legs and tossed him onto the bed, too. Violet sat on the edge and tucked her feet underneath her legs.

From the hallway, an earsplitting shriek like metal gears grinding together.

The Riders' battle cry.

2Face wanted to run. Her heart was racing, nerves twitching, veins pumping overtime. She could practically feel the adrenaline flow. She took a position to one side of the door. Raised the baseball bat over her head.

Mo'Steel stood a few feet away, pointing a BB

gun at the door. "I've been waiting for my chance at these guys," he said. "Ever since they got Errol."

Jobs crouched behind 2Face, holding a can of shaving cream. 2Face wondered how he got it out of the bathroom without getting zapped by the Squids. She wondered what he thought he was going to do with shaving cream.

Kubrick was there, too. Hovering uncomfortably close behind 2Face. He had no weapon other than his fists, which were poised and ready to strike. 2Face admired his bravery until she remembered he had never seen a Rider before. He wasn't brave. He was naive.

The door crashed inward.

A Rider appeared in the door frame. The door was wide enough for only one at a time. Good. Four of them against one Rider might just be an even fight.

The Rider's hoverboard surged forward — and stopped abruptly, jammed into the door frame, which was only inches, or fractions of inches, too small. The Rider lurched, off-balance.

"Now!" someone yelled.

Mo'Steel opened fire.

Direct hit!

The BBs sprayed into the Rider's rust-colored glossy shell. But the BBs could have been mosquito bites for all the Rider seemed to care.

He jumped off the board and bounded into the middle of the room, covering ten feet in a single leap. For a moment, the Rider paused, glaring with his two arrays of insect eyes, surveying the scene. He seemed uncertain. Anxious in this artificial, closed-in environment. He was clicking somewhere deep in his gut, communicating with the others lined up in the hallway. They clicked in response.

Another Rider appeared in the doorway. Reinforcements.

2Face raced forward, bringing the baseball bat down with all of her strength. The Rider moved sideways, missing her swing. He spun and brought up his spear.

Behind her Mo'Steel and Kubrick were shouting, apparently fighting off the next Rider.

2Face swung again, landing the bat on the four-fingered hand that clutched the Rider's spear.

Jobs let loose with the shaving cream. 2Face smelled mint, saw the lime-green foam hit the Rider in two of his smaller eyes.

He shrieked. Pain? If not pain, definitely annoyance.

"More shaving cream!" 2Face shouted.

The group on the bed was yelling, too. Cheered by this small victory.

The Rider stabbed his spear, aiming at Jobs.

2Face tried to move out of the way. She stumbled. The spear hit her in the side of the head, knocking her down on hands and knees. She looked at the carpet until her vision cleared, sucked air, looked up.

The Rider put his spear under her chin. 2Face could feel the delicate pressure there. She didn't dare move. If she moved, the Rider would decapitate her.

CHAPTER TWENTY-TWO

"LOOKS COZY ENOUGH TO ME."

The Rider froze.

At first, Violet thought it was just one of their rituals. Stillness before the kill. But the Riders in the hallway were no longer making their guttural clicking. The teddy bears were caught midsnarl and the walls had stopped exploding outward in their weird bursts.

"Looks like someone hit the pause button," Mo'Steel said, easing out of his attack stance.

Yago got up and moved closer to the Riders. "Let's just hope they stay away from rewind."

Mo'Steel helped 2Face stand. "You okay?"

2Face swallowed experimentally. She ran her hand under her chin and examined it. "I think I'm fine," she said, sounding wobbly. "What just happened?"

"We were given a chance to get out of here," Mo'Steel said. "Let's blow."

"Come on, people," Yago said. "Time for a little fresh air."

Violet noted how Yago immediately repeated any good idea, taking credit for it. He could have been trained at her mother's knee.

Edward scrambled out of the bed.

Violet got up, gently helping Alberto to his feet. Kubrick seemed happy to stay away from his father as long as someone else took care of him. At least Alberto didn't seem any worse off after the attack. He was beyond knowing what was happening around him.

The group moved out of the room, carefully easing around the wax-statue Riders. The hallway was crowded with Riders. Not the five or six Violet had imagined — dozens.

"This doesn't make sense," Jobs said as they inched along the wall toward the stairway. "Mother shouldn't be able to freeze the Riders. They're a real species, not part of her environment."

"Shh," Mo'Steel said. "They might hear you and decide to wake up and get busy with their spears. Oh, by the way, nice going with the shaving cream."

"Thanks," Jobs said, still sounding disturbed. "Hey, do you think these Riders and Squids are fake? Maybe Mother created them, knowing they scare us silly."

Jobs would turn the situation over and over until he reached some sort of conclusion that made sense to him, Violet knew. Logic was his crutch. His way of pretending this New World they'd landed in made sense. He never seemed bothered by the fact he had to keep revising his explanations — daily, even hourly.

Kubrick reached the front door first and yanked it open. "What the —" he breathed.

The weird, nightmare world they had left outside was gone. They stepped out onto the front porch and the house behind them vanished.

Violet was left in utter blackness. She couldn't feel anything, not even the ground under her feet. "Hello?" she whispered fearfully.

"I'm here," Mo'Steel whispered.

"Me, too," Jobs said.

One by one, the others answered. Kubrick reported that he had his father's arm.

Violet felt the relief flow through her. She didn't always like her companions, but having them around sure beat the horror of being alone.

A very familiar image floated into being about twenty feet away. They stood in its glow, staring at it like it was a movie screen and they were huddled down in their chairs with a Coke and a box of popcorn.

"Edward Hopper's *Nighthawks*," Violet said.

"It's a diner," Edward said. "An *old* one."

"Yes," Violet said. "Hopper painted it in the nineteen-forties. The painting is supposed to represent the sterility of modern life. See how the patrons and the waiter are all looking in different directions? They're not communicating. They're alone."

Edward was not impressed. "Looks cozy enough to me."

And it did. Maybe it was Violet's nostalgia for the lost Earth, but the darkened street with its display windows and cigar advertisements looked welcoming to her, too.

The diner itself — even more so. It was brightly lit. Not garish light, but warm like light from a fire. The patrons were enclosed within a bent glass storefront and seated on round stools at a polished wooden countertop. Everything was so neat, so orderly. The salt in its plain, functional shakers. Paper napkins in rectangular metal napkin holders. Mundane, comforting.

Then, in an instant, less so.

Two of the patrons, a pretty red-haired woman in a red dress and a somber man in a business suit and a gray fedora, disappeared. They were replaced by a young boy and what had to be an alien.

Violet turned to glance at Kubrick, to gauge his reaction. The alien — it wasn't a Rider or a Squid — had the same transparent, slick-looking skin as Kubrick.

Kubrick was leaning forward, intent but cautious. Barely breathing. He'd obviously noticed the connection, too.

The alien wore no clothes so all of its blue-tinged muscles and even a few organs were clearly visible. Violet's eyes were drawn to something large and deep green pumping in the alien's torso. A heart, perhaps.

The creature was shaped more or less like a person, but leaned short, stubby arms on the counter, wrapped four-fingered hands around a cup of what had to be coffee.

Its head was nothing but a triangular lump growing straight from the shoulders. No neck. For that matter, no mouth, nose, or ears. The head was the only part of the creature's body that wasn't transparent. Rather it was covered with milky, translucent, bumpy flesh that vibrated sensitively and continuously like a puddle on a crowded road.

On the shoulders were primitive eyes of black and red.

The boy was eight or maybe nine years old. He was very thin and pale with unruly dark hair and hollow dark eyes rimmed in red. He looked as if he hadn't had a decent meal in years — if ever. Gaunt cheeks. Bony, scabby arms.

"It's Billy," Mo'Steel whispered.

"That's right," someone said.

Violet turned at the unfamiliar voice.

It was Big Bill.

Wormholes and all.

CHAPTER TWENTY-THREE

"TWO SAD, LONELY CREATURES IN A LONELY SETTING."

"Are you real?" Jobs asked.

"No," Big Bill said, loosening his tie. He also wore a business suit and polished alligator cowboy boots. "I am a projection of Billy's imagination. He has created me to communicate with you."

"So communicate," Yago said impatiently. "What's going on in there?"

"The alien you see is a Shipwright," Big Bill said. "A Maker, one of the aliens who created this ship. To tell it true, the creature is not a true Shipwright, but a projection created by Mother. This is how Mother sees herself."

"But she's a computer," Edward complained.

"A computer," Big Bill said, "but a highly sophisticated machine. Sophisticated enough to experience loneliness, or something very close to it, when her Makers abandoned her."

Jobs and the others watched as the white-hatted waiter served Mother and Billy two steaming cups of coffee. They weren't speaking. With the Shipwright's weird eyes, Jobs couldn't even tell if they were looking at each other.

"Two sad, lonely creatures in a lonely setting," Violet said.

"And both Looney Tunes," Mo'Steel said.

"They — they seemed to be fighting before," Jobs said. "Have they reached some sort of agreement?"

"The battle continues," Big Bill said. "Only they have agreed to take it out of the realm of this node. Billy did not want all of you to die."

"How thoughtful," Yago said.

"So where are they fighting?" Mo'Steel asked.

"There at the counter," Big Bill said. "Within Billy's mind and Mother's circuitry."

Jobs felt an ache in his chest. A machine that experienced loneliness. The idea spoke to his poetic side, spoke to his techie side, spoke to all of him.

He thought of all the pain, suffering, and death that Mother's loneliness had caused. He thought of the extreme danger Billy had put himself in to try and save their lives. He'd never seen anything as sad as those two strange creatures at the diner counter.

Violet felt the sadness. He could see that on her face.

Even Alberto was slumped down, staring in the general direction of the diner. Did he recognize Mother? Recognize the machine that had been his undoing? *No,* Jobs thought. *No, that couldn't be.*

Mo'Steel and Edward were quiet, too. Awed, watching the scene unfold.

So Jobs was surprised to see 2Face approach Kubrick and strain up on her tiptoes to whisper in his ear. At first, Jobs was glad. Someone needed to talk to Kubrick, to draw him out of his anger. Maybe 2Face would know how to comfort Kubrick.

But then Jobs saw 2Face glance furtively at Yago, and he realized he was just creating pretty pictures in his head. 2Face wasn't comforting Kubrick, she was trying to win him over.

Billy and Mother may have moved their battle out of this node. But Yago and 2Face's civil war hadn't ended yet.

It hadn't *really* started.

K.A. APPLEGATE

REMNANTS™

6

Breakdown

"MOTHER WAS AS MUCH A PRISONER OF HER
PAST AS WAS BILLY."

Billy sat on one round stool, Mother on another. He rested his arms on the counter. Occasionally, he lifted a cup of coffee to his mouth and sipped. Back home, Billy had liked to drink coffee, but could do it only when his mother wasn't around. She'd said caffeine wasn't good for a growing boy.

Billy's mother, Jessica, Big Bill's wife. That was a mother, but so was the creature — or the projection — sitting next to him in the diner. A different sort of maternal figure, no doubt about that.

For one, Mother was not human. Just what she was Billy did not know, but he was learning.

Mother's projection. Her image of herself. It had the same transparent, slighty shiny skin as Kubrick.

Through the flesh, Billy could see blue-tinged muscles and viscera. He could guess the general function of some of the organs, but not many. Something large and deep green was probably the creature's heart, as it kept up a steady pumping. But that was just a guess.

The creature had a generally humanoid shape but short, stubby arms that ended in four tapered fingers, without an opposable thumb. Its legs were long and had an extra joint. The feet reminded Billy of a big bird's. There were three large toes facing forward, and one thicker toe facing backward.

Where a human's head would be the creature had a triangular protrusion growing straight from the shoulders. The head-piece reminded Billy of a starfish's arm.

The other odd thing about the creature's head was that it was not transparent but covered with milky, translucent, bumpy flesh. The flesh seemed to be a sort of supersensitive membrane. Billy watched it quiver in response to every new sound. As far as he could tell, the creature had no mouth, nose, or ears.

But it did have eyes, or what Billy thought were eyes. Small pupils in red orbs were scattered all over the creature's body, beneath the transparent flesh.

Billy noted an eye in each "shoulder," one in the palm of each four-fingered hand, one on each leg joint.

It was a Shipwright. It had to be. Billy affirmed his guess with Mother. Yes, Mother's creators. The Makers.

Where were the Shipwrights now, Billy asked. Mother did not answer.

Mother was as much a prisoner of her past as was Billy. They were two sad and lonely beings. And they were both, to some degree, insane. Billy knew this. He wondered if Mother did, too.

Billy was engaged in a battle of wills with Mother. The struggle had been fierce at first. Then Mother had ceased fighting with all her might. They were now in a benign environment Mother had pulled up from a data disc. A painting by a man named Hopper. The painting showed a brightly lit diner and three people seated at the counter. Those people had soon disappeared. They had been two-dimensional, their expressions and postures fixed.

Billy and Mother were pretty much at a stalemate. This allowed Billy a moment of relative rest and the chance to be open to what was going on with Jobs and the others.

2Face was talking low to Kubrick. Billy figured

she was considering Kubrick a potential ally against Yago.

Billy couldn't blame 2Face for politicking. Yago was selfish and intolerant. But . . . Suddenly Billy saw something else about 2Face, a memory of pain and . . . He pulled away. He couldn't concentrate on that. He'd lose his grip on Mother.

Yago was impatient and disgusted. Jobs, curious and distracted by his thoughts, as usual. Mo'Steel, nonchalant, breaking into unexplained grins. Miss Blake, the pretty, sweet one, was curious, too, but not the same way Jobs was. Little Edward was sneaking looks at Kubrick. He had been afraid of Kubrick but he wasn't anymore. Maybe he should be, Billy thought. Kubrick was consumed by anger.

And his father . . . Billy had brought his father here because he still needed Big Bill. Maybe not in the way a son usually needs his father, but that didn't matter. Big Bill was dead, Billy had helped him to die, but he was here now. In his suit and cowboy boots, his face ravished by worms.

Billy took another sip of coffee. He didn't know what would happen next. What Mother would do to him.

He hoped he would be strong enough to survive.

Because Mother had started talking again.